~ The Nutcracker ~

THE NUTCRACKER

Alexandre Dumas

Translated by
Douglas Munro

Illustrated by
Phillida Gili

London
Oxford University Press
1976

∾ For Kathryn ∾

25864

Oxford University Press

OXFORD LONDON GLASGOW NEW YORK TORONTO MELBOURNE WELLINGTON CAPE TOWN
IBADAN NAIROBI DAR ES SALAAM LUSAKA ADDIS ABABA KUALA LUMPUR SINGAPORE
JAKARTA HONG KONG TOKYO DELHI BOMBAY CALCUTTA MADRAS KARACHI

ISBN 0 19 271379 5

First published in Paris in 1844 in 'Le Nouveau
Magasin des Enfants' in 40 parts under the title
of *Histoire d'un Casse-Noisette*, to appear in book
form under the same title in 1845, Paris, 'publié par
J. Hetzel', with woodcut illustrations by Bertall.

© English translation by Douglas Munro 1976
Illustrations © 1976 by Phillida Gili
First published in this edition 1976

PRINTED IN AUSTRIA

∾ Translator's Note ∾

You will all, I think, know the music of Tchaikovsky's 'Nutcracker Suite'. But do you know that the ballet was based to a great extent on Dumas' story? The ballet, in fact, does not include anything about Princess Pirlipatine and the Krakatuk nut. Dumas' work is an adaptation, freshly told in his own inimitable way, of E. T. A. Hoffmann's *The Nutcracker and the Mouse King*—he has enhanced it greatly.

Douglas Munro

～ Chapter One ～

There lived in Nuremberg, many years ago, a man of great respectability named Judge Silberhaus. The judge had a son and a daughter; the son was nine years old and was called Fritz, and the daughter who was seven and a half was named Marie. They were good-looking children, but so different in character and appearance that no one would have believed them to be brother and sister.

Fritz was a well-built boy, with ruddy cheeks. He was impatient and stamped on the floor when he could not get his own way, for he thought that everything had been made for his own amusement or to suit him. He would stay in one of his moods until the judge, annoyed by his cries and screams or by his stamping, came out of his study and raising his forefinger said, 'Fritz!' This was quite enough to make Fritz wish that the earth would open and swallow him up. As for his mother, it didn't matter how much or how often she raised her forefinger for Fritz took not the slightest notice of her.

His sister, on the contrary, was a pale and delicate girl with long hair curling naturally and flowing over her shoulders like a flood of golden light. She was bashful yet friendly, and always kind, even to her dolls. She was very obedient to her mother and never contradicted her governess, Miss Trudchen. In fact, Marie was loved by everyone.

Now, at the time of this story, 24 December had arrived. You will probably know that Nuremberg is a town famous for its toys, puppets and Punch and Judy shows. It can be well imagined that the children of Nuremberg should be the happiest in the world. Every country at Christmas has its own customs and Christmas Eve in Germany is the great day for giving presents. Moreover, in Germany children's presents are given in a special way; some sort of tree is stood upon a table in the sitting-room and on all its branches are hung the toys that are to be distributed. Playthings that are too heavy to hang on the tree are put around it on the table, and the children are told that it is their guardian angel who has sent them all these lovely presents. And that is a harmless enough deception, after all.

It need scarcely be said that among the children of Nuremberg who received most presents were the son and daughter of Judge Silberhaus for, besides their father and mother who doted on them, they also had a godfather who loved them dearly, and whose name was Drosselmeyer.

Something should be said here about this famous man who held in the town of Nuremberg almost as high a position as that of Judge Silberhaus himself. Drosselmeyer was a doctor and was not by any means a very good-looking man. He was thin and tall, nearly six feet high, but stooped so badly that in spite of his long legs he could almost pick up his handkerchief if it fell without stooping any further. His face was as wrinkled as an apple that has withered and fallen from the tree. Being blind in the right eye he wore a black patch, and being quite bald he wore a shining and frizzled wig which he had made himself from glass. For fear of damaging this amazing contrivance he always carried his hat under his arm. His other eye was sparkling and bright, and seemed not only to do its own work but also that of its absent companion, so rapidly did it take in everything that was in a room or fix itself upon a person whose secret thoughts Drosselmeyer wished to read.

It may seem curious, but the learned doctor was not like other physicians who look after people who are ill—he occupied his time in giving life to dead things. Through his studies he had gained a deep knowledge of how bones worked, and he fashioned men who could walk, bow to each other, and go through their exercises with a musket. He also made ladies who danced, and played on the harp and violin; dogs that ran and barked; birds that flew, hopped and sang; fish that swam and swallowed crumbs of bread. He had even made puppets who could speak a few words. The sounds that were made by all these things were monotonous and harsh, because it can be very well understood that they were produced by means of machinery concealed inside the toys.

With his knowledge of mechanical things Drosselmeyer was a most useful man to his friends. For instance, if a clock belonging to Judge Silberhaus went out of order, if the hands suddenly stopped, if the tick-tock seemed to go badly, or if the wheels inside would not move, the good doctor was at once sent for, and he hurried to the house as quickly as he could, for he was an artist devoted to his craft.

He was no sooner shown the poor clock than he instantly opened it to take out the works and put them between his knees. Then, with his tongue sticking out a little, his eye glittering, and his wig laid upon the floor, he would take from his pocket a number of little tools which he had made himself and the proper use of which he alone knew. Choosing the sharpest one he would plunge it into the very midst of the works, to Marie's great alarm for she could not believe that the poor clock did not suffer from such an operation. But in a short while when the old man had touched the works in various places and put them back in their case the clock soon began to revive, to tick as loud as ever, and to strike clearly at the proper time, and thus give new life to the room itself which without it seemed a melancholy place.

Moreover, to please Marie who was sad to see the kitchen dog, Turk, turning the spit, Drosselmeyer made a mechanical wooden dog which could do the work. Turk, who had carried out this duty for three years until he had become quite shaky all over, was now able to lie in peace in front of the kitchen fire and amuse himself by watching the movements of his successor. So, after the judge, after the judge's wife, and after Marie, the dog Turk was certainly the next inmate of the house who had reason to love and respect Drosselmeyer. Turk was indeed grateful and showed his gratitude whenever Drosselmeyer was nearing the house by leaping up against the front door and wagging his tail even before the old gentleman had knocked.

On the evening of this 24 December then as twilight was getting nearer, Fritz and Marie who had not been allowed in the sitting-room all day were huddled together in a corner of the dining-room. Their governess was knitting near the window, to which she had moved her

3

chair in order to catch the last rays of daylight. The children were filled with a vague wonder because candles had not been brought into the room according to the usual custom, and they were talking in low voices to each other.

Night fell and almost at once a bell rang, the door was thrown open and so strong a light burst into the room that the children were dazzled. Then the judge and his wife appeared at the door, saying:

'Come, see what your guardian angel has sent you.'

Fritz and Marie rushed into the sitting-room. A great tree seemed to be growing from the middle of the table, covered with flowers made from sugar, and sugar-plums instead of fruit—the whole glittering by the light of a hundred Christmas candles hidden among the branches and leaves. Their joy knew no bounds when they came to examine all the lovely things which covered the table. Among all else there was a large and beautiful doll for Marie, and Fritz found a squadron of hussars with red jackets and gold lace mounted on white horses, while on the carpet there stood a wooden horse which he had so much longed for.

The bell rang a second time, and the children turned towards the corner of the room from which the sound came. The corner was cut off by a large Chinese screen from behind which there was the sound of music and this reminded them, somehow or other, that they had not yet seen the doctor. They both exclaimed at the same moment: 'Oh, where is godfather Drosselmeyer?'

At these words, as if it only waited for them to be said, the screen opened and showed not only Doctor Drosselmeyer but something more. In the middle of a meadow dotted with flowers stood a magnificent castle with any number of windows made of real glass in the front and two handsome gilded towers at each wing. And just then the ringing of tiny bells was heard, the doors and windows opened and the rooms inside could be seen lit up by wax tapers half an inch in length. In the rooms were a number of little men and women, all walking about. The men were splendidly dressed in lace coats and silk waistcoats and breeches, each with a sword by his side and a hat under his arm; the women were beautifully attired in brocades, each one dressed in the manner of Madame de Pompadour, and each one holding a fan in her hand, and they all fanned themselves as if overcome by the heat.

In the large central room, which could have seemed to be on fire so

4

bright was the reflected light from the crystal chandelier filled with wax candles, a number of children were dancing to the jingling music, the boys all in short jackets and the girls all in long frocks. At the same time a man dressed in a fur cloak appeared at the window of a neighbouring room, made signs, and then disappeared again, while a puppet only three inches high exactly like Drosselmeyer himself with his yellow frock-coat, the patch over his eye and the glass wig, went in and out of the front door of the castle with the air of a man inviting those outside to come in.

The first few minutes were full of surprise and delight for the children, but after a while Fritz, who had been leaning on his elbows on the table, stood up and exclaimed:

'But, godfather Drosselmeyer, why do you keep going in and coming out of the same door? You must be tired of going backwards and forwards like that. Come, enter by that door there, and come out by this one here.'

And Fritz pointed to the doors of the two towers.

'No, that cannot be done,' Drosselmeyer answered.

'Well, then,' Fritz went on, 'do me a favour by going up those stairs and taking the place of the man at the window, and then tell him to go down to the door.'

'It is impossible,' the doctor replied.

'In any case, the boys and girls have danced enough. Let them go and walk while the grown-ups do some dancing instead.'

'You are not being reasonable, you little rogue,' cried the doctor, who was beginning to grow angry. 'The mechanism must work in a certain way.'

'Then let me go into the house,' Fritz said.

'Now you're being silly,' his father interrupted, 'you can see very well that it is impossible for you to enter the castle since the tops of the towers scarcely come up to your shoulders.'

Fritz gave in after that and remained quiet. But a little later seeing that the men and the ladies kept on walking, that the children did not stop dancing, that the man in the cloak appeared and disappeared at regular intervals, and that Doctor Drosselmeyer went on going in and out of the door, he said in a disillusioned voice:

'Godfather, if all these little figures can do nothing more than that

6

over and over again you can take them away tomorrow, for I am not interested in them. I like my horse and my hussars because they can move as I want them to do and are not shut up in any house like your poor little people who can only move all the time in the same way.'

And with these words he turned his back on Doctor Drosselmeyer, went to the table, and arranged his soldiers in battle array.

As for Marie she had slipped away quietly because the movements of the little figures seemed to her to be very tiresome, but she said nothing for fear of hurting her godfather's feelings. Indeed, the moment Fritz had turned his back the doctor said crossly to the judge and his wife:

'This masterpiece is too good for children. I am going to put it back in its box and take it home.'

But the judge's wife came over to him, and to make up for her son's rudeness begged him to explain all the secrets of the beautiful castle, and praised it so much that she not only made the doctor forget his annoyance but put him in such good humour that he took from his coat pockets a number of little figures brown in colour, with white eyes and gilded hands and feet. Besides being lovely to look at they gave forth a delicious perfume because they were made of cinnamon.

Just then the governess called Marie to help her put on a pretty silk dress which was one of her presents. But Marie, in spite of her usual politeness, did not answer for she was so much occupied with a new discovery among the toys, a personage who is the principal figure in what follows.

∾ Chapter Two ∾

By making his hussars march and countermarch across the table Fritz
had brought to light a little man who was leaning, and looking melancholy, against the trunk of the Christmas-tree, waiting silently and
patiently, and very politely, for when his turn to be examined arrived.
His body was too long and big for the miserable little thin legs which
supported it, and his head was so enormous that it was out of all propor-
tion to the rest.

   He wore a braided frock-coat of violet-coloured velvet, all frogged
and covered with buttons, and trousers of the same material, as well as
shiny boots. But there were two things which seemed strange compared
with the rest of his dress—one was an ugly narrow cloak made of wood
which hung down rather like a pigtail from the nape of his neck to the
middle of his back, and the other was a wretched little cap, such as some
mountaineers wear, upon his head. But Marie, when she saw these two

oddities which seemed so out of keeping with the rest of his dress, remembered that her godfather himself wore on top of his yellow frock-coat a collar of no better appearance than the wooden cloak belonging to the little man, and that the doctor often covered his own bald head with an ugly cap quite unlike all other ugly caps in the world.

Marie liked this quaint little man from the first moment she saw him. The more she looked at him the more she was struck by the sweetness and amiability of his face. Although rather goggle-eyed he beamed with serenity and calmness through his green eyes; the frizzled beard of white cotton seemed to become him amazingly because it set off the charming smile of his mouth, which was rather wide perhaps, but then the lips were vermilion red.

After examining the little man for almost ten minutes, without daring to touch him, Marie asked her father who he was for.

'He belongs to no one in particular,' the judge replied, 'but to both of you. This fellow will help you both, for it is he who in future will crack all your nuts for you. He belongs as much to Fritz as to you, and as much to you as to Fritz.'

Having said this the judge picked up the little man very carefully, and lifting his wooden cloak made him open his mouth to display two rows of sharp, white teeth. Marie then put a nut in his mouth, and crack— crack—the shell was broken into pieces and the almond fell whole into her hand. She was then told that this dandified gentleman belonged to that ancient and respectable race of nutcrackers whose origin was as ancient as that of the town of Nuremberg, and that he continued to exercise the honourable calling of his forefathers.

Marie, delighted with what she had learned, jumped for joy, and the judge then said:

'Well, Marie, since the nutcracker pleases you so much and although he belongs equally to you and your brother, it is to you that I especially entrust him. I put him in your care.'

And he handed the nutcracker to her. Marie chose the smallest nuts so that he might not have to open his mouth too wide, because if he did so his face assumed a most ridiculous expression.

When he heard the crack—crack being so often repeated Fritz felt sure that something new was going on, and he looked up from his hussars. He joined in the fun and, despite his sister's protests, chose the largest and hardest nuts to cram into the nutcracker's mouth. So, at the fifth or sixth c-r-r-ack, out fell three of the poor little fellow's teeth. At the same time his chin fell and became tremulous like that of an old man.

'Oh, my poor nutcracker!' Marie cried, snatching him from Fritz.

'What a stupid fellow he is!' the boy shouted. 'He pretends to be a nutcracker, and his jaws are as brittle as glass. He is a false nutcracker and doesn't understand his duties. Give him back to me and I'll make him go on cracking nuts even if he loses all his teeth in doing so and his jaw is dislocated.'

At Marie's cries the judge and his wife and Doctor Drosselmeyer came to see what was the matter. The two children told their own stories, Marie wanting to keep the nutcracker and Fritz anxious to have him again. To Marie's astonishment the doctor, with a smile that seemed frightening to her, decided in the boy's favour. But luckily for the poor nutcracker the judge and his wife took Marie's part.

'Fritz,' said the judge, 'I placed the nutcracker in Marie's care, and I can see that the poor creature is very unwell and needs attention. From now on he belongs entirely to Marie. You, with your love of soldiers, when did you ever hear of making a wounded man return to battle?'

Fritz was about to reply, but the judge raised his forefinger to the level of his right eye and said, simply, 'Fritz!'

It has already been told what happened when Fritz was spoken to in this way; he went quietly away, without giving any answer, to the table where his hussars were paraded, and having mounted his sentries marched the rest off to their quarters for the night.

Marie picked up the three little teeth that had fallen out and wrapped up the nutcracker in a large handkerchief after binding up his chin with a ribbon. For his part the little man, who was at first very pale and frightened, seemed quite contented in the care of his protectress and gradually gained confidence when he felt himself being rocked gently in her arms.

Then Marie noticed that her godfather watched with a mocking smile the care that was being given to the little man in the wooden cloak, and it seemed to her that the doctor's single eye had an expression of spite and malice she had never seen before. She started to go away, but the doctor burst out laughing, saying:

'Well, my child, I am really astonished that a pretty little girl like you can be so devoted to this frightful little man.'

Marie turned. She was angry, and the vague comparison which she had before formed between the little man with the wooden cloak and her godfather returned to her memory.

'Godfather, you are unkind towards my poor little nutcracker whom you call frightful. I wonder whether you would look as handsome as he does if you were wearing his frock-coat, his breeches, and his beautiful boots!'

When they heard this Marie's parents burst out laughing, and the doctor's nose grew astoundingly longer.

Why did the doctor's nose grow so much longer? Marie, surprised by the effect of her remark, certainly did not know.

∾ *Chapter Three* ∾

To the right of the judge's study was a cupboard with glass doors in which the children's toys were kept. It had been made by a very skilful cabinet-maker who had put such sparkling glass in the frames that the toys appeared ten times more beautiful when ranged on the shelves than when one was holding them. Upon the topmost shelf, which neither of the children could reach, were placed the lovely pieces of workmanship fashioned by Doctor Drosselmeyer. Below that was the shelf holding their picture-books, and the two lowest shelves were given over to the toys, which they arranged as they liked best.

There seemed to be a mutual understanding between the pair of them that Fritz should have the higher shelf for the billeting of all his soldiers, and that Marie should keep the bottom shelf for her dolls and their dresses. An agreement had been reached on Christmas Eve—Fritz should arrange his soldiers on his own shelf and Marie should put her dolls to bed and leave them with a dish of sugar-plums in case they woke up hungry during the night.

While all this was being done the evening wore away. Midnight was coming nearer—Doctor Drosselmeyer had been gone a long time—and yet the children could not be persuaded to leave the cupboard. Contrary to custom it was Fritz who first finally agreed to go to bed, but only after he had given his hussars the watchword to prevent them from being surprised by an enemy. Marie pleaded to stay up a little longer and her mother agreed, but thinking that her daughter might forget to put the candles out she did this, leaving only a light in the lamp hanging from the ceiling.

The moment Marie found herself alone she went to her poor little nutcracker who was still wrapped up in a handkerchief. Very gently she put him on a table, unrolled the handkerchief, and examined his chin. The nutcracker still seemed to be in pain and appeared to be very cross.

'Oh, my poor little fellow,' she said softly, 'don't be angry because my brother hurt you so much. He didn't really mean to, even though he handled you so roughly. I will take care of you and in a few days you will be quite well again. As for putting your teeth in again and fastening your chin properly that is the business of Doctor Drosselmeyer who perfectly understands things of this kind.'

Marie could not go on talking to him, for the moment she mentioned Doctor Drosselmeyer's name the nutcracker made such a dreadful face, and his eyes suddenly flashed so brightly, that she stopped short and stepped quickly back. But as the nutcracker almost immediately resumed his amiable expression and his sad smile she thought that she had been imagining things, that possibly the flame from the lamp had flickered and in that way had changed the appearance of the little man.

She even laughed at herself, saying, 'I am very stupid to think that this wooden puppet could make faces at me.'

So Marie picked up the nutcracker, went to the cupboard, knocked at the glass door, and told her new doll that as the poor nutcracker was unwell she would have to give up her bed to him for the night and sleep on the sofa. At this the doll looked sulky and discontented, but with no more ceremony the nutcracker was put into bed and the bedclothes tucked up to his chin. Marie then lifted the bed with the nutcracker in it on to the second shelf close to the village where Fritz's hussars were quartered, put the doll on a sofa, closed the cupboard and started to go to her bedroom.

Suddenly she heard any number of soft scratching sounds coming from behind the chairs, the stove and the cupboard. The large clock which hung on the wall and which had on its top a gilt owl, instead of a cuckoo as is usual with old German clocks, gave a whirring sound. Marie glanced towards it and saw that it had drooped its wings in such a way that they covered the entire face of the clock. Then the whirring of the clock became louder and louder and gradually changed to sound like a human voice, and to say:

'Clocks, clocks, whirr, whirr, softly. The king of the mice has a sharp ear. Sing him his old song. Strike, strike, clocks, sound his last hour—for his fate is near.'

And then, boom, boom, boom, the clock struck twelve in a muffled, hollow tone.

Marie was rather frightened and was about to run from the room when she saw, or thought she saw, godfather Drosselmeyer seated on the clock instead of the owl, his coat-tails having taken the place of the drooping wings of the bird. She called out to him: 'What are you doing up there, godfather? Come down here and don't frighten me like that, you naughty godfather.'

But at these words there began a sharp whistling and an angry twittering all around, and in a few moments Marie heard numberless little feet treading behind the walls; next she saw tiny lights through cracks in the wainscoting—but the lights were little eyes. In the course of five minutes what seemed to be hundreds of mice had made their appearance and ranged themselves in battle order, just as Fritz liked to draw up his toy soldiers. All this seemed very amusing to Marie who was not one bit alarmed.

There suddenly rang through the room a long, curious whistling noise and, at the same time, a floorboard was lifted by some power underneath—and the king of the mice, with seven heads each wearing a golden crown, appeared at her very feet. The entire army marched towards the king and then across the floor to the cupboard. Marie was standing close to it and, quite by accident, broke one of the panes with her elbow. The mice disappeared, scared she thought by the noise of the breaking glass. But almost at once there was a strange noise in the cupboard and a number of voices called out:

'To arms! To arms!'

At the same time the music in Doctor Drosselmeyer's castle, which had been placed on the top of the cupboard, began to play, and from all sides she heard:

'Quick, get up, it is the enemy! To arms!'

Marie turned round. The cupboard was lit up in a wondrous way, and all was bustle within. All the harlequins, the clowns, Punch, and the other puppets scampered about, hurrying here, hurrying there, encouraging the others, while the dolls set to work to make lint and prepare bandages for the wounded. Finally the nutcracker threw off his blankets and jumped out of bed shouting:

'Foolish mice, return to your holes or you will have me to deal with!'

But at that another whistle echoed through the room and Marie saw that, frightened by the noise of the breaking glass, the mice had taken refuge beneath chairs and tables, and had now begun to form their battle-lines again. For his part, the nutcracker far from being alarmed by this fresh whistle, seemed to gather fresh courage.

'Miserable king of the mice!' he exclaimed. 'It *is* you then. Come, let this night decide between us. And you, my good friends, my companions, support me in this perilous contest! Let those who love me follow me!'

Never did such a proclamation produce such an effect. Two harlequins, a clown, Punch, and three other puppets answered in one loud voice:

'Yes, my lord, we are yours in life and death! We will conquer under your command, or die with you!'

Hearing this the nutcracker became so excited that he drew his sword and without realizing the dreadful height on which he stood leapt from his shelf. Marie, seeing that dangerous leap, gave a cry, for the nutcracker seemed on the point of being dashed to pieces, but the new doll who was on the lower shelf darted from her sofa and caught him in her arms. She said to him:

15

'What! My lord—wounded and suffering as you are, you are plunging headlong into new dangers. Content yourself with commanding the army, and let the others fight! Your courage is known and you can do no good by giving fresh proof of it!'

The doll, who by the way was called Claire, tried to restrain the gallant nutcracker by holding him tight in her arms, but he began to kick and struggle so much that she was forced to let him go. He slipped from her arms and fell on his knees at her feet in a most graceful manner, saying:

'Princess, although once you were unjust to me, I shall always remember you even in the midst of battle.'

Claire stooped as low as she could and taking him by his arm raised him to his feet. She then took off her waist-band, all glittering with spangles, and made a scarf of it to go over his shoulders. But the nutcracker stepped back a few paces, bowed in acknowledgement of so great a favour, untied the white ribbon with which Marie had bound up his chin, kissed it, and tied it about his waist.

Then, light as a bird, he jumped from the shelf to the floor and brandished his sword when he had safely landed. Immediately the squeakings and creaking began all over again, and more fiercely than before. The king of the mice, as if to reply to the nutcracker's challenge, came out from under the table in the middle of the room followed by the main body of his army. At the same time the right and left wings of the army began to appear from beneath the armchair under which they had taken refuge.

~ *Chapter Four* ~

'Trumpets, sound the charge! Drums, beat the alarm!' the nutcracker shouted.

And at once the trumpets of Fritz's hussars rang forth, while the drums of his infantry began to beat, and the rumbling of cannon wheels was also heard. At the same time a military band was somehow formed and their music doubtless roused the peaceably-minded toys, for a kind of home-guard assembled made up of harlequins, clowns and jumping-jacks. Arming themselves with anything they could lay their hands on they were soon ready for the battle. All was astir, even to a cook who leaving his fire came down with his spit, on which was a half roasted turkey, to take his place in the ranks. The nutcracker took his place at the head of this valiant band which, to the shame of the regular troops, was ready first.

If Fritz's infantry and cavalry were not ready as soon as the others it was only because they were all shut up in four boxes and couldn't get out, even though they could hear the trumpets and drums calling on them to fight. Marie could hear them stirring in their boxes and at length the grenadiers less firmly shut up succeeded in raising the lids of their boxes, and they then helped to free the light infantry. These, in turn, knowing well how useful cavalry is in a battle, released the hussars who began to canter about and range themselves four deep upon the flanks.

The regular troops quickly made up for lost time. Infantry, cavalry and artillery began to descend with the fury of an avalanche amid the applause of the two dolls, who clapped their hands as they passed and encouraged them by calling out to them.

Meantime the king of the mice saw that he had to fight an entire army. The nutcracker was in the centre with his gallant home-guard; on the left was the regiment of hussars awaiting only the moment to charge; on the right was a formidable battalion of infantry; while, upon a foot-stool which commanded the whole scene of battle, stood a battery of ten cannons. In addition to all these there was a powerful reserve made up of gingerbread men and warriors made of different coloured sugar which had stayed behind in the cupboard but which were already beginning to bustle about. The king of the mice had, however, advanced too far to be able to retreat, and he gave the signal by a squeak which was repeated by all the forces under his command.

The battery on the footstool replied with a volley of shot and the hussars charged. With the dust raised by the horses' feet and the smoke from the cannons Marie could not follow the battle, but she could hear the nutcracker's voice above the din.

'Sergeant Harlequin,' he shouted, 'take twenty men and fall upon the enemy's flank! Lieutenant Punch, form into a square! Captain Puppet, fire in platoons! Colonel of hussars, charge in masses and not four deep as you are doing! Bravo, my good soldiers, if all my troops behave as well as you the day is won!'

The mice thrown back returned again and again to the charge. It was like the combats in the days of chivalry, a furious hand-to-hand struggle, each bent on attack or defence without waiting to think of his neighbour. The nutcracker vainly tried to direct matters. The hussars were scattered and failed to rally round their colonel, for a battalion of the enemy had cut them off from the main body of the army and had actually advanced as far as the home-guard, which was performing prodigies of valour— the cook was actually running ranks of mice through with his spit!

Sergeant Harlequin and his twenty men had been driven back and forced to retreat under cover of the battery; Lieutenant Punch's square had been broken and his troops had fled, to throw the home-guard into disorder. Captain Puppet's platoon, doubtless for want of cartridges, had ceased to fire and was in full retreat. As the result of this retreat along the line, the battery of cannon was exposed, and the king of the mice seeing that success depended on its capture, ordered his bravest troops to attack it. The footstool was stormed and the artillerymen were cut to pieces by the side of their cannon. One of them set fire to his powder-wagon and met an heroic death with twenty of his enemies.

But all this courage was useless against such numbers, and very soon a volley of shot fired upon them from their own cannon and which swept the forces commanded by the nutcracker, revealed to him that the footstool was in the hands of the enemy.

From then on the battle was lost, and the nutcracker now thought only of beating an honourable retreat. To give his troops breathing time he summoned the reserves to his aid. At once the gingerbread men and the coloured sugar warriors descended from the cupboard and gave battle in their turn. They were certainly fresh, but very inexperienced, troops. The gingerbread men especially were very awkward, and, hitting right and left, they did as much injury to friends as foes. The sugar warriors stood firm, but they were all so different—emperors, knights, Tyroleans, gardeners, cupids, monkeys, lions and crocodiles—that they could not combine their movements and were strong only as a mass. Their arrival, however, did some good, for scarcely had the mice tasted the ginger-bread men and the sugar warriors than they left the soldiers, whom they found difficult to bite, and turned away also from the harlequins, Punch and the cook who were only stuffed with sawdust, to fall upon the unfortunate reserve which was all finally eaten up.

Nutcracker tried again to rally his army, but the destruction of the reserve had struck terror into the bravest hearts. Captain Puppet was as pale as death; Harlequin's clothes were in rags; a mouse had bitten Punch's hump; and not only was the colonel of hussars a prisoner but the mice had even formed a squadron of cavalry with the captured horses. The unfortunate nutcracker now had no chance of victory, he could not even retreat with honour, so he placed himself at the head of a small body of men determined like him to sell their lives dearly.

Meanwhile, terror remained among the dolls who wrung their

hands, their cries mingling with their tears. Matters went from bad to worse with the nutcracker for he was abandoned by the few friends who had remained faithful to him. What was left of the squadron of hussars took refuge in the cupboard; the soldiers had all fallen into the enemy's hands; the artillery had long since dispersed; while the home-guard had been cut to pieces, like the three hundred Spartans of Leonidas, without yielding a step.

The nutcracker stood at bay against the lower part of the cupboard which he vainly sought to climb. But he could not do so without the help of the dolls, who had found nothing better to do than faint. He made a last effort, collected all his strength, and cried in an agony of despair:

'A horse! A horse! My kingdom for a horse!'

But as with Richard III his voice remained without even an echo, or rather betrayed him to the enemy.

Two of the rifle-brigade of the mice seized on his wooden cloak, and at the same time the king of the mice cried out:

'On your heads, take him alive! Remember that I have my mother to avenge! His punishment must serve as an example to all future nutcrackers!'

And with these words the king rushed upon the prisoner.

But Marie could no longer bear to watch.

'Oh, my poor nutcracker!' she exclaimed. 'I love you with all my heart and cannot bear to see you die!'

At that very moment, instinctively and without knowing what she was doing, Marie took off one of her shoes and threw it with all her strength. Her aim was so good that the shoe hit the king of the mice and made him roll over in the dust. Then the king and army, conquerors and conquered, all vanished as if by magic. Marie felt a more severe pain than before in her arm and she tried to reach an armchair to sit down. But her strength failed her and she fainted.

∾ *Chapter Five* ∾

When Marie awoke from a deep sleep she found herself lying in her bed with the sun shining radiant and brilliant through the hoar-frosted windows. At her side sat someone whom she soon recognized as their family doctor, and who said in a quiet voice as soon as she opened her eyes, 'She is awake.'

Then her mother came over to the bed and gazed at her daughter anxiously.

'Oh, mother,' Marie said, 'are all the mice gone and was my poor nutcracker saved?'

'My dear Marie, do not repeat all that nonsense. What have mice, I should like to know, to do with the nutcracker? But you have given us an awful fright. You played with your toys very late last night. You most likely fell asleep, and it is probable that a little mouse wakened you and scared you. At any rate you pushed your elbow through one of the panes of the cupboard and cut yourself badly. Thank goodness I woke up during the night and, remembering how I had left you in the room, went down to see if everything was all right. You were stretched on the floor near the cupboard and all around were strewn the dolls, the puppets, the soldiers, the gingerbread men and the hussars—all scattered about pell-mell—while in your arms you held the nutcracker. But how did it happen that you had taken off one of your shoes and that it was lying some distance away from you?'

'Mother,' said Marie, shuddering as she thought of what had happened, 'all that you saw was the result of the great battle that took place between the toys and the mice. When I saw the victorious king of the mice about to seize the poor nutcracker, who was in command of the toys, I threw my shoe at him. After that I don't know what happened.'

'Forget all that, Marie, all the mice are gone and the little nutcracker is safe and comfortable in the cupboard.'

Marie saw at once that her story was not believed; she didn't say anything more but allowed everyone to have their own way. She was anxious to get up as soon as possible and pay a visit to her nutcracker now that she knew he had escaped safe and sound from the battlefield. That was all she cared about for the present.

But time hung very heavily on her. She couldn't play because of her wounded arm and she looked forward to the evenings because her mother would then come and sit by her and read stories to her. One evening the judge's wife had just ended the tale of Prince Facardin when the door opened and Doctor Drosselmeyer looked in. When Marie saw him with his glass wig, his black patch, and his yellow frock-coat, the memory of the night when the nutcracker lost the famous battle against the mice returned so forcibly to her mind that she could not stop herself from crying out:

'Oh, godfather Drosselmeyer, you really were very ugly! I saw you quite clearly when you sat on top of the clock covering it to stop it from striking because it would have frightened the mice away. Why didn't you come to help my poor nutcracker? By not coming you were the cause of my hurting myself and having to stay in bed.'

The judge's wife listened to all this in amazement, and said in low voice:

'What *are* you talking about, Marie? Are you taking leave of your senses?'

'Oh, no,' Marie answered, 'and godfather Drosselmeyer knows that I am telling the truth.'

But Doctor Drosselmeyer didn't say a word until all of a sudden he recited in a sing-song voice:

'Clock chime, beat
Low, dull and hoarse;
Advance, retreat,
You gallant force.
The chime's low sound proclaims around
The hour of deep midnight,
And the piercing note from the screech-owl's throat
Puts the king himself to flight.
Clock chime, beat
Low, dull and hoarse;
Advance, retreat,
You gallant force.'

Just as he finished, Fritz entered the room with a shout, saying:
'That song of yours, godfather Drosselmeyer, doesn't make sense.'
And the judge's wife, looking severe, added:
'My dear doctor, your song is indeed very strange.'
'Nonsense!' Doctor Drosselmeyer answered. 'Don't you recognize
the clockmaker's song that I'm in the habit of humming when I come to
mend your clocks?'
He then came and sat down beside Marie and said to her:
'Don't be angry with me because I didn't scare the mice away. I knew
what I was about and now, as I am anxious to make it up with you, I will
tell you a story.'
'What story?' Marie asked.
'The story of the Krakatuk nut and Princess Pirlipatine. Do you
know it?'   ·
'No,' Marie answered, whom the offer of a story made her friends
again with the doctor. 'Go on, please.'
'My dear doctor,' said the judge's wife, 'I do hope that your story will
not be as melancholy as your song.'
'Oh, no,' Doctor Drosselmeyer replied. 'On the contrary, it is very
amusing.'
Both the children called out to him to begin, and this was his story.

∾ *Chapter Six* ∾

There was not so long ago, quite near Nuremberg, a little kingdom which was not Prussia, nor Poland, nor part of the Palatinate. The king's wife, who was therefore a queen, became the mother of a little girl, who was of course a princess, and who was to be christened Pirlipatine.

When the king was told of the great event he hurried very out of breath to see the child in her cradle. The joy that he felt on being the father of so delightful a child carried him to such a length that, quite forgetting himself, he uttered loud cries of joy and began to dance around the room, ending up by hopping on one foot and calling out:

'Oh, who has ever seen anything so beautiful as my Pirlipatine!'

Then, as the king had been followed by his ministers, his generals, his great officers of state, his chief judges and his counsellors, they all began dancing round the room behind the king, singing:

'No, no, never, your majesty, has there ever been born anything so beautiful as your Pirlipatine!'

And indeed, although it may surprise you to be told so, there was not a word of flattery in this, for no lovelier child than Princess Pirlipatine had ever been seen. Her face seemed to be made of the softest silk, her eyes were of the purest and brightest blue, and her golden hair held promise of delicate curls. Moreover, and remember this, Pirlipatine was born with two rows of the most pearly teeth with which, two hours after her birth, she bit the finger of the lord chancellor so hard when, being short-sighted, he stooped down to look closely at her, that he cried out, 'Oh, the deuce!'; although some said that he simply muttered under his breath, 'Oh, Oh.' Opinions are divided on this important subject, neither party being willing to yield to the other, but the people soon knew that the charming Pirlipatine had as much spirit as beauty.

Everyone in the kingdom was happy except the queen, who was anxious and uneasy, and no one knew why. What most struck people with surprise was the care with which the mother had the cradle watched. In fact, besides having all the doors guarded by soldiers, in addition to the two regular nurses the queen had six other nurses to sit around the cradle whose places were taken by half a dozen others at night. But what caused the greatest interest, and which no one could understand, was that each of these six nurses had to nurse a cat and to stroke it all night so that it wouldn't stop purring. The reason for this must be explained.

It happened one day that half a dozen great kings took it into their heads to pay a visit to the future father of Princess Pirlipatine, for at that time the princess had not yet been born. With them came the royal princes, the heirs apparent, and the grand dukes, all most agreeable people. Their arrival was the signal for the king, who was a most hospitable monarch, to spend a very great deal of money, and to give tournaments and feasts. But this was not all. He learned from the chef of the royal kitchens that the astrologer-royal had announced that the moment was favourable for the killing of pigs, and that the stars foretold that the year would be an excellent one for the making of sausages.

The king commanded that a great many pigs should be killed and then, ordering his carriage, called personally on all the kings and princes staying in his capital to invite them to dine with him, for he was determined to surprise them by the splendid banquet he intended to give them. On his return to the palace he went to the queen's apartment and going up to her said in a coaxing voice which he always used when he wanted her to do something special for him:

'My very dear one, you have not forgotten, have you, how much I love black puddings? You surely have not forgotten that?'

The queen knew at once what the king wanted of her—she knew that she must now go, as she had done so many times before, to the very useful occupation of making with her own royal hands the greatest possible quantity of black puddings and sausages. So she smiled at what her husband said for, although filling with dignity her high position as queen, she was less sensible of the compliments paid to her when she bore the sceptre and the crown than of those bestowed on her skill in making a black pudding or some such similar dish. She therefore curtsied grace-

26

fully to her husband and said that she was only too pleased to make him the black puddings and sausages that he wanted.

The grand treasurer was accordingly given orders to deliver to the royal kitchens the immense enamelled cauldron and the large silver saucepans so that the queen might get on with her cooking. A big fire was made with sandalwood, the queen put on her kitchen apron of white damask, and in a short time the most delicious smell was coming from the cauldron: this spread along the corridors, quickly penetrated all the rooms and finally reached the throne-room where the king was holding a counsel.

The smell made a profound impression on him. As he was a wise man and famed for his self-control he resisted for a long time the itch which attracted him towards the kitchens, but at last in spite of the command which he exercised over himself he just had to give in.

'Gentlemen,' he said, rising from his throne, 'with your permission I will retire for a minute or two. Do, please, wait for me.'

Then he hurried through the rooms and along the corridors to the kitchens, embraced his wife tenderly, stirred what was in the cauldron with his gold sceptre, took a taste of what was cooking, and having thus calmed his mind he returned to the counsellors and resumed, although rather abstractedly, the subject under discussion.

He had left the kitchen just at that moment when the fat, cut into small pieces, was about to be broiled on the silver grids. The queen, encouraged by his praise, now started on this important business, and the first drops of grease had just dripped on the live coals when a squeaking voice was heard to say:

'My sister, please give to the queen of the mice
A piece of that fat which is grilling so nice;
To me a fine dinner is something so rare
That I hope of the fat you will give me a share.'

The queen recognized at once the voice that was speaking, it was that of Dame Souriçonne who had lived for many years in the palace. She claimed to be a relation of the royal family and was queen of her kingdom, maintaining a large court behind the kitchen fire-place.

Although she did not recognize Dame Souriçonne as a sister and a

27

sovereign, the queen was a kind and good-natured woman and gave her, in private, a number of small favours. The king, more particular than his wife, had often reproached her for thus lowering herself. But on this occasion she could not find it in her heart to refuse the request of her little friend and she said:

'Come, little mouse, have no fear. Taste my pork fat as much as you like, you have my permission to do so.'

The mouse, gay and lively, accordingly jumped on the hearth and took with her paws the pieces of fat which the queen gave her. But her little cries of joy and the delicious smell of the morsels of fat reached the ears and noses of her seven sons, then her relations, and next her friends, all of whom were hearty eaters and who fell upon the fat so greedily that the queen was obliged, hospitable as she was, to remind them that if they continued at that rate there would not be enough fat left for the black puddings. But in spite of this warning the mice took no notice, and the fat would have been entirely eaten up had not the cries of the queen brought the chef and the cook's boys, all armed with brushes and brooms, to drive the mice back again behind the hearth.

But the victory, although complete, came a little too late, for there scarcely remained a quarter enough fat necessary for the black puddings, let alone the sausages. What was left, however, was scientifically divided by the royal mathematician, who was sent for in all possible haste, between the cauldron holding the makings of the puddings and the two saucepans in which the sausages were cooking.

Half an hour later a cannon was fired, clarions and trumpets were sounded, and there then arrived the potentates, the royal princes, the hereditary dukes, and the heirs apparent, all dressed in their most splendid clothes. Some travelled in crystal coaches, others rode on lovely horses. The king received them on the palace steps in the most courteous possible manner. He then conducted them to the banqueting-room and took his seat at the head of the table wearing his crown and holding his sceptre. The guests all took their places according to their rank.

The table was laid out magnificently, and everything went well during the soup and the next course. But when the sausages were served the king went very pale; when the black puddings were brought in he raised his eyes to heaven, sighed heavily, and a terrible grief seemed to

rend him. Finally he fell back in his chair and covered his face with his
hands, sobbing and moaning in such a way that all the guests rose from
their seats and surrounded him with great anxiety. His attack seemed to
be very serious; the court physician could not find the pulse of the unfortunate monarch who seemed to be overwhelmed by the most profound, most frightful, and most unheard of calamity.

At last, after the use of the severest remedies such as burnt feathers

held under his nose, smelling-salts, and keys pushed down his back, the
king seemed to recover. He opened his eyes and said in a scarcely audible
voice, '*Not enough fat.*'

At these words the queen went pale in her turn. She went down on her
knees to him and said in a voice interrupted by sobs:

'Oh, my unhappy, unfortunate and royal husband! What grief I have
caused you by not listening to the advice which you have so often given
me! But you see the guilty one at your feet, and you can punish me as
you think fit!'

'What's the matter?' demanded the king. 'What has happened that you have not spoken to me about it?'

'Alas!' the queen answered, for the king had never spoken so crossly to her before. 'Alas, Dame Souriçonne, her seven sons, her nephews, her cousins and friends, ate most of the fat.'

The queen could not say any more; her strength failed her and she fell back in a faint.

Then the king rose in a great rage and cried in a terrible voice:

'The royal housekeeper must explain all this!'

The royal housekeeper told all she knew, that being alarmed by the queen's cries she ran and saw her majesty surrounded by the whole mouse family and that, having summoned the chef and the cook's boys, the plunderers were driven away behind the hearth.

The king, realizing that this was a case of high treason, resumed all his dignity and calmness and commanded his counsellors to meet that very minute. They assembled, the business was explained, and it was decided by a large majority that Dame Souriçonne, having been accused of eating the fat meant for the sausages and black puddings of the king, should be tried for that offence; further, if she should be found guilty, she and all her race should be banished from the kingdom and all their goods and chattels should be taken from them.

The king then remarked that while the trial lasted, Dame Souriçonne and her relations and friends would have had enough time to eat up all the fat in the royal kitchens, which would expose him to the same privation as that which he had just suffered in the presence of six crowned heads, not to mention the royal princes, hereditary dukes, and heirs apparent. The counsellors took a vote, just for the form of the thing, and the discretionary powers that the king wanted were, as may be well imagined, voted again by a large majority.

There was then sent, at the king's express command, one of his best carriages, which was preceded by a courier for greater speed, to a very skilful craftsman who lived in Nuremberg and whose name was Christian Elias Drosselmeyer. This craftsman was requested to come to the palace with all possible speed on a matter of urgency. Christian Elias Drosselmeyer immediately obeyed, for he felt sure that the king was wanting him to make some work of art. He got into the carriage and travelled day and night until he arrived in the king's presence.

30

Indeed, such was his haste that he had not had the time to change the yellow frock-coat that he always wore. But, instead of being angry at this breach of etiquette, the king was much pleased with his haste, for if the famous craftsman had committed a fault it was in his anxiety to obey the king's command.

The king led Christian Elias Drosselmeyer to his private study and explained the situation to him, namely, that it was decided to make an example of the mice by driving them all out from his kingdom, and knowing of his fame and skill the king had chosen him to execute justice. The king's only fear was lest the craftsman, skilful as he was, would meet insurmountable difficulties in appeasing the royal anger.

But Christian Elias Drosselmeyer reassured the king and promised him that in a week there would not be a single mouse left in the kingdom.

That very same day he set to work to make a number of ingenious little oblong boxes, inside which he placed a morsel of fat on the end of a piece of wire. By biting the fat the thief, whoever he might be, would make the door shut down behind him and would thus become a prisoner. In less than a week a hundred of these boxes were made and put not only behind the hearth but in all the cupboards and cellars of the palace.

Dame Souriçonne was far too wise not to discover at first glance Drosselmeyer's stratagem. She therefore called before her her seven sons, her nephews and cousins to warn them of the trap that was being laid for them. But, after having seemed to take heed of her because of the respect they held for her and the veneration which her years commanded, they went away laughing at her fears. Then, attracted by the smell of the cooked pork-fat, they decided in spite of what they had been told to profit from the windfall that had come to them.

At the end of twenty-four hours the seven sons of Dame Souriçonne, eighteen of her nephews, fifty cousins, and two hundred and thirty-five of her other relations, without counting thousands of other mice, were caught in the traps and ignominiously killed.

And so, Dame Souriçonne, with the remnant of her race, decided to abandon a place where there had been so much bloodshed. This news soon became known and reached the king's ears. His majesty expressed great satisfaction and the court poets wrote sonnets on his victory, while the courtiers compared him with Alexander the Great and Julius Caesar.

The queen alone was anxious and uneasy. She knew Dame Souriçonne well and had no doubts that she would not leave unavenged the deaths of her sons and relations. In fact, at the very moment when the queen by way of atonement for her previous fault was preparing with her own hands some liver soup for the king, a dish that he doted upon, Dame Souriçonne suddenly appeared and spoke to her as follows:

'Your husband, bereft of pity and fear,
Has killed sons, cousins and nephews dear;
But tremble, oh queen, to this decree of fate,
The child which will soon be given to thee,
And which the subject of your love will be,
Will bear the rage of my vindictive hate.

Your husband owns castles, cannon and towers,
Has counsellors' wisdom and an army's powers,
Ministers, craftsmen, mousetraps and snares;
None of these, alas, can to me belong
But heaven has given me teeth sharp and strong
That I may bite very sharply all royal heirs.'

Having recited this, Dame Souriçonne disappeared, and no one saw her afterwards. But the queen, who was expecting her first child, was so overcome by what she had heard that she upset the liver soup into the fire.

So, for the second time, Dame Souriçonne was the cause of depriving the king of one of his favourite dishes, and although he fell into a dreadful rage he was more than ever delighted with the steps he had taken to rid his kingdom of the mice.

It goes without saying that Christian Elias Drosselmeyer was splendidly rewarded and returned in triumph to Nuremberg.

∾ *Chapter Seven* ∾

So it can be well understood why the queen had Princess Pirlipatine so carefully watched. She dreaded the vengeance of Dame Souriçonne. And what increased the queen's fears was that the traps invented by Drosselmeyer were absolutely useless against the person of the very knowledgeable and practical Dame Souriçonne.

The court astrologer was afraid that his office might be abolished unless he gave his opinion at this particularly grave time. He accordingly said that he had read in the stars the important fact that the illustrious family of the cat called Murr was alone capable of defending the princess's cradle. It was for this reason that each of the six nurses had to hold a cat constantly in her lap. These cats were attached to the court as lap-warmers-in-ordinary, and the nurses undertook to lighten the burden of their duties by gently stroking them.

But there are certain times when people doze off in spite of themselves, and so it happened one evening that despite all their efforts the six nurses felt drowsy. Now, as each nurse kept her own feelings to herself and hoped all the time that her drowsiness would not be noticed by the others, the result was that one after the other they closed their eyes, their hands stopped stroking the cats, and the cats, being no longer stroked, decided to go to sleep too.

It cannot be said for certain for how long their slumbers lasted, but somewhere about midnight one of the nurses woke with a start. All the others were sound asleep, and not a sound, not even their breathing, could be heard. Then the nurse was very frightened to see a large mouse sitting up near her on its hind legs and then jump into the cradle. She jumped up with a cry of alarm which awakened the other nurses, and Dame Souriçonne, for she it was, sprang from the cradle towards a corner of the room. The cats leapt after her. But it was too late, she had disappeared through a hole in the floor.

At the same moment Princess Pirlipatine, who was awakened by all the din, began to cry. At the sound of this the nurses uttered exclamations of joy.

'Heaven be praised,' they said, 'if the princess cries she cannot be dead.'

They all rushed to the cradle, but their exclamations of joy gave place to cries of dismay when they saw what had happened to the charming little princess. Instead of having a pink and rosy face with blue eyes and golden hair she had suddenly become a very unattractive shrivelled little thing with scarcely any resemblance to the quite adorable child that the king and queen, and everyone else in the palace, had known and loved.

Just then the queen entered the room. The six nurses went down on their knees, and the six cats stalked about to discover whether there was an open window through which they could escape to the tiles. At the sight of the child the poor queen fainted and had to be carried to the royal bedchamber. But it was the unhappy king whose sorrow was the most desperate and painful to see. He ate nothing for the three following days, saying without ceasing:

'Oh, unfortunate king that I am! How cruel is fate!'

Perhaps instead of accusing fate he should have remembered that he was really the cause of his own misfortunes. For had he been content with his black puddings containing a little less fat than usual, and had he given up his ideas of vengeance and left Dame Souriçonne and her family in peace under the hearth, all this unhappiness would not have occurred. But it must be admitted that the father of Princess Pirlipatine didn't think of that.

34

Instead, believing as great men are inclined to do, that they must attribute their misfortune to others, he threw all the blame on the craftsman Drosselmeyer. Quite sure, too, that if he invited him back to court to be hanged or beheaded he would not accept the invitation, he asked him to come so that he might receive a new order of knighthood which had just been created for men of letters, artists and craftsmen. Drosselmeyer was not free from human pride; he thought that a ribbon would look well on his yellow frock-coat and, accordingly, at once set out. But his joy was soon changed to fear, for on the kingdom's frontier guards awaited him. They seized him and under escort he was taken to the capital.

The king, who was afraid that in the end he might be tender-hearted, would not see Drosselmeyer when he arrived at the palace. Instead, he ordered that he should be led at once to Princess Pirlipatine's cradle and be told that if the princess were not restored to her original beauty by a month from that day then he would be beheaded without mercy.

Drosselmeyer had no pretence to heroism and had always hoped to die a natural death. He was, therefore, much frightened at this threat. Nevertheless, relying on his scientific knowledge which his modesty had never prevented him from being aware of, he plucked up courage. Then he set to work to discover whether the princess was really incurable, as he was at first inclined to believe.

With a wonderful dexterity he first of all examined the princess's head, and then all her limbs and joints and muscles. But the longer he probed and worked the more firmly convinced did he become that her appearance could not be changed. So he put Pirlipatine back in the cradle again and sitting beside her he fell into the most melancholy thoughts.

The end of his time to cure Pirlipatine wore on, and on a Wednesday in accordance with his usual custom the king called to see if there were any progress. But when he saw there was no change he shook his sceptre at Drosselmeyer and cried:

'You had better take care! You have only three days left to restore my daughter to how she used to look, and if you stay obstinate in refusing to cure her on Sunday next you will be beheaded!'

Drosselmeyer, who could not cure the princess because of any obstinacy on his part but through ignorance of how to do it, began to weep bitterly. As he did so he noticed through his tears that the baby was cracking a nut as happily as if she were the most beautiful child in the world. He was then struck for the first time by the particular love of nuts which she had shown since the day she was born, and he remembered, too, the quite remarkable fact that she was also born with teeth. In fact, immediately after her change from beauty she had begun to cry loudly until she found a nut within reach; she then cracked it, ate the kernel, and turned over to go quietly to sleep. From then onwards the nurses had taken good care to fill their pockets with nuts and gave her one whenever she made a face.

'Oh, nature, wonderful nature!' Drosselmeyer called out. 'You have shown me the door which leads to your secrets, and I will knock at it and it will open!'

With these words, which greatly surprised the king, Drosselmeyer turned towards him and requested the favour of being taken to the court astrologer. The king consented but on the condition that a guard should go with him. Drosselmeyer would have been better pleased to take that little walk by himself but as in the circumstances he could not disobey orders but must do as he was told, he walked through the streets of the capital like any common criminal.

On reaching the astrologer's house Drosselmeyer threw himself into his arms and they embraced, for they were old friends and much attached to each other. They then retired to a private room and examined a great number of books which dealt with a great number of subjects. At last night fell. The astrologer climbed up to his tower and with the help of Drosselmeyer, who was himself very skilled in such matters, discovered that, in spite of the difficulties of the orbiting of the planets which crossed one another's paths in all directions, to break the spell which bound Princess Pilipatine and to restore her to her former beauty she must eat the kernel of the Krakatuk nut, the shell of which was so hard that the wheel of a forty-eight pounder cannon might pass over it without breaking it.

Further, it was necessary that this nut should be cracked in the presence of the princess and by a young man who had never shaved and had always worn boots. Lastly, it was necessary that he should present the kernel to the princess with his eyes closed, and in the same way step seven paces back without stumbling. Such was the answer of the stars.

Drosselmeyer and the astrologer had worked without ceasing for three days and three nights to clear up this mystery. On Saturday evening —the king had nearly finished his dinner and was just beginning the dessert—Drosselmeyer entered the royal dining-room full of joy to announce that he had discovered the way to restore the princess's beauty. Hearing this the king took him in his arms with the most touching kindness, and asked how it was to be done.

Then and there Drosselmeyer explained to the king the result of his consultation with the astrologer.

'I knew perfectly well, Drosselmeyer,' the king said, 'that all your delay was only through obstinacy. It is, however, settled at last and as soon as I have finished dinner we will set to work. Be very careful, my good fellow, to have the young man who has never been shaved and who has always worn boots in readiness in ten minutes along with the

37

Krakatuk nut. Tell him not to drink any wine just now in case he should stumble while walking backwards like a lobster. But you can say to him that when everything is over he is welcome to the freedom of my cellar to drink as much as he likes.'

But to the king's great astonishment Drosselmeyer seemed quite frightened at these words, and as he stayed silent the king insisted upon knowing why he held his tongue and remained standing instead of hurrying to carry out the orders given to him.

'Your majesty,' said Drosselmeyer, kneeling, 'it is perfectly true that we have found the means of curing Princess Pirlipatine, but we have not as yet either the Krakatuk nut or the young man. We do not know where to find either of them and probably we will have the greatest difficulty in doing so.'

Hearing this the king was furious and brandishing his sceptre over Drosselmeyer's head he shouted:

'Very well then, get ready to die!'

But, for her part, the queen hurried to kneel beside Drosselmeyer and begged her august husband to remember that by cutting off his head he would be losing even that ray of hope which remained to them. The chances were, she insisted, that he who had found the answer to their problem would also find the nut and the young man, that although up to now nothing that the astrologer had predicted had ever come to pass there was always the chance of a first time, and they ought to believe in him more firmly, particularly as the king had quite recently given him the title of 'Grand Augurer'.

The queen went on to say that as the princess was not yet of an age to marry (she was now only three months old) and would not reach that age until she was fifteen, there were, therefore, fourteen years and nine months during which Drosselmeyer and his friend the astrologer might search for the Krakatuk nut and the young man who was to break it. She thus suggested that a reprieve should be given to Christian Elias Drosselmeyer, at the end of which he should return to surrender himself to the king whether he had found the means of curing the princess or not. He should then either be generously rewarded or put to death on the spot.

The king, who was a very just man, and who that day had dined splendidly upon his two favourite dishes of liver soup and black pudding,

38

gave a favourable ear to the words of his wise and magnanimous queen. So he decided that Drosselmeyer and the astrologer should at once set out in search for the nut and the young man, for which purpose they would be given fourteen years and nine months on the condition that they should return then and place themselves in his hands, so that if they were empty-handed he might deal with them according to his own royal pleasure.

But if they should reappear with the Krakatuk nut the astrologer would be rewarded with a yearly pension of a thousand thalers and a telescope of honour; Drosselmeyer would receive a sword set with diamonds and the Order of the Golden Spider, which was the highest order in the kingdom, and a new frock-coat.

As for the young man who was to crack the nut, the king had no doubts about being able to find a suitable candidate by advertising regularly in the national and foreign newspapers.

Touched by the generosity of the king, which relieved them of half the difficulty of their task, Christian Elias Drosselmeyer gave his word of honour that he would either find the Krakatuk nut or return, like another Regulus, to place himself at the disposal of the king.

That very same evening the astrologer and Drosselmeyer departed from the capital of the kingdom to start their search.

~ *Chapter Eight* ~

Fourteen years and five months had passed since the astrologer and Drosselmeyer first set out on their wanderings without discovering anything like that which they sought.

They had first of all travelled through Europe, then America, next Africa, and afterwards Asia. They even discovered a fifth part of the world which learned men later called New Holland. But throughout their long series of travels, although they had seen many nuts of different shapes and sizes, they never came across the Krakatuk nut. In vain hope they had spent several years at the courts of the King of Dates and the Prince of Almonds; they had uselessly consulted the celebrated academy of the green monkeys, and the famous naturalist society of squirrels, until at length, drooping with fatigue, they arrived at the borders of the great forest which stretches to the feet of the Himalayas. And now they said sadly to each other that they had only about one hundred and twenty days to find what they sought.

40

If all the strange adventures which happened to the two travellers during that long wandering were to be told it would occupy every evening for a month, and would be wearisome. It should, however, be said that Christian Elias Drosselmeyer, who was the most eager in the search for the famous nut since his head depended on the finding of it, gave himself up to greater dangers than his companion, and lost all his hair as a result of sunstroke in the tropics. He also lost his right eye by an arrow which a Caribbean chief fired at him. Moreover, his yellow frock-coat, which was not new when he set out, had literally fallen into tatters. His circumstances, therefore, were most deplorable and yet, damaged as he was by the accidents which had happened to him, so much does a man cling to life that he saw with increasing terror the approach of the day when he must return to put himself in the king's hands.

He was a man of honour and could not break any promise that he had made. He accordingly decided that whatever the cost he would immediately return to Europe. He made his intentions known to the astrologer and the travellers resumed their journey at daybreak, taking the direction of Baghdad. From Baghdad they went to Alexandria, whence they sailed to Venice. From Venice they passed through the Tyrol and from there they entered the kingdom of Princess Pirlipatine's father, both sincerely hoping that he was either dead or in his dotage.

But no such luck! When they reached the capital the unfortunate Drosselmeyer learned that the worthy monarch not only had not lost his mental faculties but was, indeed, in better health than ever. There was thus no chance of him escaping his fate unless the princess had been transformed without any remedy at all, which was not possible, or that the king's heart had softened, which was not probable.

Drosselmeyer nonetheless went boldly with the astrologer to the gates of the palace and asked permission to speak to the king. The king, who was easy of access, ordered the grandmaster of ceremonies to bring the strangers into his presence. The grandmaster replied that the strangers were of a most villainous appearance and could not possibly be worse dressed. But the king answered that it was wrong to judge the heart by the face, and that clothes did not make the man. The grandmaster saw the justice of these observations, bowed respectfully, and went to fetch Drosselmeyer and the astrologer.

The king was the same as ever and they at once recognized him. But the travellers were so changed, especially poor Christian Elias Drossel-meyer, that they were obliged to say who they were. Seeing that the two had returned of their own accord the king gave a sigh of joy, for he felt quite sure that they would not have come back if they had not found the Krakatuk nut. But he was quickly disillusioned when Drosselmeyer, throwing himself at the king's feet, confessed that in spite of the most earnest and constant search they had returned empty-handed.

As is known, the king, although temperamental, was an excellent man at heart. He was touched by the punctuality with which Christian Elias Drosselmeyer had kept his word and he changed the sentence of death to one of life imprisonment; as for the astrologer he contented himself by sending him into exile.

But there were still three days remaining of the period of fourteen years and nine months' allowance of time granted by the king, and Drosselmeyer who was deeply attached to Nuremberg implored permission to spend those days there. This request seemed so reasonable that the king granted it even without attaching any promise of return.

Drosselmeyer found that there were two empty seats on the mail-coach and at once reserved them. As the astrologer had been sentenced to exile, and it was all the same to him where he went, he left with Drosselmeyer. Next morning, at about ten o'clock, they were in Nuremberg and as Drosselmeyer had only one relation in the world, his brother Christopher Zachariah who kept one of the main toyshops in the town, it was at his home that they alighted.

Christopher Zachariah was overjoyed to see his brother Christian Elias whom he believed to be dead. First of all he found it difficult to believe that the man with the bald head and the black patch over one eye was, in fact, his brother; but when he was shown the famous yellow frock-coat which, tattered as it was, had kept in some places traces of its original colour, and when some family secrets were mentioned to him he was quickly reassured. He then inquired of his brother what had kept him so long absent from his native town, and in what country he had lost his hair, his eye, and the missing pieces of his frock-coat.

Christian Elias had no reason to keep secret from his brother the events which had occurred. He began by introducing his companion in misfortune, and he then related what had happened from start to finish, ending by saying that he had only a few hours to spend with his brother because, not having found the Krakatuk nut, he was on the point of being shut up in a dungeon for ever.

While Christian Elias was telling his story Christopher Zachariah had more than once twiddled his thumb, turned about on one leg, and clicked his tongue. In other circumstances Christian Elias would have asked his brother what he was doing but he was so full of his own thoughts that he said nothing. It was only when his brother exclaimed 'Hum! Hum!' twice, and 'Oh! Oh! Oh!' three times that he asked the reason for these exclamations.

'The reason is,' said Christopher Zachariah, 'that it would be strange indeed if.. but, no .. and yet ...'

'What do you mean?' Christian Elias asked.

'If ...' continued the toy-merchant.

'If what?'

But instead of answering, Christopher Zachariah threw his wig into the air and began to caper about. Then he said:

43

'My brother, you are saved! You won't go to prison, for unless I am much mistaken I have a Krakatuk nut.'

And without further explanation to his astonished brother, Christopher Zachariah rushed out of the room, to return in a minute with a box containing a large gilded filbert which he handed to him.

Christian Elias, who dared not believe in such good luck, rather hesitantly picked up the nut and turned it over and over to examine it with all the attention it deserved. He then declared that he was of the same opinion as his brother and that he would be very much astonished if the filbert were not, indeed, the Krakatuk nut. He then handed it to the astrologer for his opinion. The astrologer examined it as closely as Christian Elias had done, but shaking his head replied:

'I would also be of the same opinion as the two of you if the nut were not gilded, for I have seen nothing in the stars showing that the nut we have searched so hard for should be so ornamented. Besides, how did your brother come by the nut?'

'I will explain everything to you,' Christopher Zachariah answered. 'I will tell you how the nut came into my hands and how it came to have that gilding which is an obstacle to its being fully recognized and which, indeed, is not its own naturally.'

Then having insisted on them sitting down, for he very wisely thought that after travelling for fourteen years and nine months, except for a couple of days, they must be tired, he went on:

'On the same day as the king sent for you under the pretence of giving you an order of knighthood a stranger arrived in Nuremberg carrying a sack of nuts which he wanted to sell. But the nut merchants of the town, anxious to keep to themselves the monopoly of this foodstuff, quarrelled with him outside my shop. The stranger, to defend himself the more easily, put his bag of nuts on the ground and the quarrel went on to the great delight of the small boys and other onlookers, when the wheels of a heavily laden wagon went over the sack.

'When the merchants saw what had happened, and they put it down to the justice of heaven, they considered themselves properly avenged and left the stranger in peace. He picked up his sack and found all his nuts to have been crushed except one which he handed to me with a curious sort of smile, asking me to buy it from him for a new zwanziger piece dated 1720. He said that the day would come when I would not regret the bargain, dear as it might then seem. I felt in my pocket and was most surprised to find a coin with exactly that date. The coincidence seemed so strange that I gave it to him, and he handed me the nut and went away.

'I put the nut in my window for sale and although I asked only a couple more kreutzers than I paid for it, it stayed in the window for seven or eight years without anyone wanting to buy it. I then had it gilded to increase its value, and that cost me another two zwanzigers—money wasted, for the nut as you see was never sold.'

Just as he finished speaking, the astrologer, in whose hands the nut had remained, gave a cry of joy. While Christopher Zachariah had been talking, the astrologer had delicately scraped off some of the gilding on the nut and had found on it the word KRAKATUK engraved in Chinese characters.

There could be no doubt about it—the identity of the nut had been established.

～ Chapter Nine ～

Christian Elias Drosselmeyer was in such a hurry to give the good news to the king that he wanted to return by the mail-coach at once, but Christopher Zachariah persuaded him to stay until his son returned home. Christian Elias agreed, particularly since he had not seen his nephew for fifteen years.

A little later a good-looking young man of about eighteen or nineteen entered and was introduced to his uncle and told to shake hands with him. The youth hesitated, for his uncle with his frock-coat in tatters, his bald head, and the patch over his eye did not seem to be a very attractive person. His father noticed his hesitation and fearing that his brother's feelings would be hurt pushed his son forward.

While the introduction was being made the astrologer gazed so steadily at the young fellow that the latter became ill at ease and as soon as he could left the room. The astrologer at once asked a number of questions from which it transpired that his mother had taken a delight in dressing him when he was young like some of the puppets which her husband sold, as a student, as a postilion, or in Hungarian national dress, but always in such a way that he must wear boots.

'And so,' said the astrologer to Christopher Zachariah, 'your son has always worn boots?'

Christian Elias opened his eyes wide.

'My son has never worn anything but boots. When he was ten I sent him to Tubingen University, where he remained until he was eighteen without contracting any of the bad habits of his companions such as drinking, swearing and brawling. The only weakness of which he is guilty is that he allows four or five wretched hairs which he has on his chin to grow. He won't let any barber touch them.'

'So your son has never been shaved?'

'Never.'

'And how did he pass his time during the vacations?' continued the astrologer.

'He helped in the shop, and out of pure good nature cracked nuts for all the young ladies who came in to buy toys and who, because of this, nicknamed him "Nutcracker".'

'Nutcracker?' his brother cried out.

'Nutcracker?' repeated the astrologer.

And then they looked at each other while Christopher Zachariah looked at them both.

'My dear sir,' said the astrologer, 'in my opinion your fortune is as good as made.'

Naturally Christopher Zachariah wanted an explanation, but the astrologer, however, put this off until next morning.

When Christian Elias and the astrologer were shown to their room the astrologer embraced his friend and said:

'It is he! We have found him!'

'Do you think so?' asked Christian Elias in the tone of a man who is doubtful but only waits to be convinced.

'Can there be any doubt? He has never worn anything but boots, he has never been shaved, and what's more he has stood in his father's shop to crack nuts for customers who never called him anything else but "Nutcracker".'

'All that is very true.'

'My dear friend,' went on the astrologer, 'one stroke of good luck never comes alone. But if you are still doubtful let us go and consult the stars.'

They accordingly went on to the roof of the house, and having drawn the young man's horoscope discovered that he was destined to great good fortune. This prediction confirmed all the astrologer's hopes, and Drosselmeyer was forced to come to the same opinion.

'And now,' said the astrologer triumphantly, 'there remain only two things to be done. The first is that, somehow, you must fix a strong piece of wood to your nephew's neck and connect it in such a way with the lower jaw that the utmost power will be exerted.'

'Nothing could be simpler,' answered Christian Elias.

'The second thing,' continued the astrologer, 'is that on arriving at the palace we must carefully conceal the fact that we have brought with us the young man who is destined to crack the Krakatuk nut. My opinion is that the more teeth there are broken, and the more jaws there are dislocated in trying to break the nut, the more eager the king will be to increase the reward to whoever succeeds.'

'My dear friend,' replied Christian Elias, 'you are a man of sound sense. Let us go to bed.'

And with these words they went down to their bedroom where, having pulled their cotton nightcaps over their ears, they slept more peacefully than they had done for nearly fifteen years.

Early next morning the two friends went to the apartment of Christopher Zachariah and told him all the fine plans they had formed the evening before. Now, as the toy-merchant was not wanting in ambition, and as he flattered himself that his son must have the strongest jaws in all Europe, he willingly agreed to the arrangement whereby there was taken from his shop not only the nut but also the nutcracker.

The young man himself was more difficult to persuade. The piece of wood which was to be fitted to his neck particularly worried him, but his father, his uncle, and the astrologer made him such splendid promises that he finally fell in with their wishes. Christian Elias went to work at once, the wooden balance was made and was so firmly fixed to his neck that the young man was now full of hope. It should be mentioned here that the ingenious contrivance worked so perfectly that with the first trials the young protegé was able to crack the hardest apricot stones and the most obstinate peach stones.

The trio then at once set out for the king's palace. Christopher Zachariah was anxious to accompany them but as he had no one to look after his shop he resigned himself to remaining behind at Nuremberg.

48

~ *Chapter Ten* ~

The first care of Drosselmeyer and the astrologer on reaching the capital was to leave the nephew at the inn where they were staying and then go to the palace to announce that, having vainly sought the Krakatuk nut all over the world, they had in fact found it in Nuremberg. As had been agreed between them they did not mention who it was who would crack the nut.

The gladness at the palace was very great. The king at once sent for the privy counsellor who looked after the information services and who also acted as a censor of the newspapers. This important man, at the king's command, wrote an article for *The Gazette* which all other newspapers were ordered to copy, to the effect that those who fancied that they had teeth strong enough to break the Krakatuk nut were to present themselves at the palace and, if anyone were to be successful, he would be liberally rewarded for his trouble.

This was an unparalleled opportunity to show how rich the kingdom was in strong jaws. The candidates were so many that the king was forced to form a committee, the chairman of which was the royal dentist, and its duty was to examine all the competitors to see if they had all their thirty-two teeth and that none were decayed.

Three thousand five hundred candidates were admitted to the first trial, which lasted a week, and which resulted only in an unknown number of broken teeth and dislocated jaws.

It was therefore necessary to make a second appeal, and all national and foreign newspapers were filled with advertisements. The king offered the post of life-president of the Royal Academy together with the Order of the Golden Spider to whoever should succeed in cracking the nut. There was no need to have a university degree to stand as a candidate.

This second trial produced five thousand candidates. All the learned societies of Europe sent their representatives to this important gathering. Several members of the French Academy were present as well as the permanent secretary of that institution, but he was declared *persona non grata* because all his teeth had long since been broken in his frequent attempts to tear to pieces the works of his brother authors. This trial, which lasted a fortnight, was as fruitless as the first. The deputies of the learned societies argued among themselves, for the honour of the societies to which they belonged, as to who first should crack the nut, but in the end they only left their best teeth behind them.

As for the nut itself its shell did not even bear the marks of the attempts that had been made to crack it.

The king was in despair. He decided to make a final attempt to find someone who would be successful. As he had no sons he announced by means of a third article in *The Gazette*, the national newspapers, and the foreign journals, that the hand of Princess Pirlipatine and the inheritance to the throne would be given to the man who cracked the nut. There was one condition—the candidates must be between sixteen and twenty-four years old.

The promise of such a reward caused tremendous excitement. Competitors poured in from all parts of Europe, and they would even have come from Asia, Africa, America, and that fifth part of the world which had been discovered by Drosselmeyer and his friend the astrologer but for the fact that time was limited. It was just then that the pair of them thought that the moment was favourable to produce their prodigy, for it

50

was impossible for the king to offer any higher reward.

But, certain of success as they were, and although this time a host of princes had presented their royal jaws, they did not appear with their young friend at the office for registering applications until it was just about to close. The name of Nathaniel Drosselmeyer was numbered 11,375 on the list, and was the last.

There was no difference between this third trial and the preceding ones. The 11,374 rivals of young Nathaniel failed, and on the nineteenth day of the contest, and at twenty-five minutes to twelve on the morning of the princess's fifteenth birthday, the name of Nathaniel Drosselmeyer was called.

The young man presented himself accompanied by his two guardians. It was the first time that these two illustrious men had seen the princess since she was in her cradle. The years had not improved her, and on seeing her, poor Nathaniel shuddered and asked his uncle and the astrologer if they were quite sure that the kernel of the Krakatuk nut would restore the princess to her beauty. He went on to say that if she were to remain as unattractive as she now was he was perfectly prepared to do what others had failed to do, but he would leave the honour of marriage and the inheritance of the throne to anyone who might be inclined to accept them.

It is hardly necessary to say that both Drosselmeyer and the astrologer hastened to reassure him and to affirm that the nut once broken, and the kernel once eaten, Pirlipatine would instantly become the most beautiful princess in the world.

But if the sight of Princess Pirlipatine had struck Nathaniel with dismay it must be said that the sight of him had produced a very different effect on the sensitive heart of the princess. She could not stop herself from exclaiming:

'Oh, how I wish so much that he would break the nut!'

To which the chief governess of the princess replied:

'I think I have often observed to your highness that it is not customary for a young and beautiful princess like yourself to express such opinions aloud.'

Nathaniel could, indeed, be reckoned to turn the heads of all the princesses in the world. He was wearing a violet velour military frock-coat, braided, and with gold buttons, which his uncle had made. His breeches were of the same material, and as for his boots they shone like mirrors.

The only thing that rather spoiled his appearance was the piece of wood fitted to his neck. His uncle had tried to so fashion it that it seemed rather like a small cloak attached to his wig; at a stretch it might have passed as an eccentricity in the young man's dress, or else as a new fashion which his tailor was trying to put into vogue at the court.

And so when this charming young man entered the room what the princess had had the imprudence to say aloud the other ladies present said to themselves. There was not a single person, not even the king and queen, who did not wish from the bottom of their hearts that Nathaniel might prove triumphant in the venture which he had undertaken.

For his part young Drosselmeyer showed his confidence and this encouraged the hopes that were placed in him. Having reached the steps leading to the throne he bowed first to the king and queen, and then to Princess Pirlipatine, and finally to the spectators. When he was given the Krakatuk nut by the grand master of ceremonies he held it delicately between his forefinger and thumb, put it between his teeth, and gave a violent pull at the piece of wood attached to his neck.

Crick! Crack! And the shell was broken into several pieces.

He then skilfully separated the kernel from the fibres hanging to it and presented it to the princess, bowing gracefully and respectfully to her as he did so. The princess immediately bit the nut, chewed it, and swallowed it and, wonderfully, all her plainness at once disappeared and she became a young lady of infinite beauty. Her face seemed to have borrowed the pinkness of a rose and the whiteness of a lily, her eyes were a sparkling blue, and the thick tresses of her golden hair flowed over her lovely shoulders.

The trumpets and the cymbals sounded and they made enough noise to deafen one, while the cries of the audience mingled with the noise of the instruments. The king, the ministers, the counsellors of state, and the judges began to dance, as they had done at the birth of Princess Pirlipatine, and eau-de-cologne had to be sprayed over the queen's face for she had fainted with joy.

All this tumult proved to be very annoying for young Nathaniel Drosselmeyer who, it will be remembered, had yet to step seven paces back. However, he behaved with perfect coolness and was just stretching

52

out his leg to take the seventh step when Dame Souriçonne suddenly appeared through a crevice in the floor. With a squeak she ran between his legs so that just at the very moment when the future prince royal put his foot down, his heel came on to the body of the mouse, and he stumbled as if he were about to fall.

At that very same moment the handsome young man was transformed; his legs shrivelled, his shrunken body could hardly support his head, he became goggle-eyed and his eyes turned green, his mouth opened from ear to ear, and his delicate little sprouting beard changed into something white and soft which was afterwards found to be cotton-wool.

But the cause of this transformation was punished, for Dame Souriçonne was dying—young Drosselmeyer had stepped on her so hard that she was crushed beyond all hope of recovery. Even so she was able to squeak as follows:

> 'Krakatuk, krakatuk, fatal nut and so hard,
> Through you my life has been finally marred,
> But the queen of the mice has thousands to back her
> And my son will yet punish the wretched nutcracker.
> I know! I know!'

Dame Souriçonne's verse might have been better but it must be admitted that in the circumstances she was at a distinct disadvantage. A high officer of the court picked her up by the tail and she was taken away to be buried in the hole where so many of her family had been buried fifteen and more years earlier.

In the middle of all this no one had particularly troubled themselves about Nathaniel Drosselmeyer except his uncle and the astrologer. The princess, who was unaware of the accident that had happened, ordered the young hero to be brought to her presence, for in spite of what her governess had said she was in a great hurry to thank him. But scarcely had she seen the unfortunate Nathaniel than she buried her face in her hands. Forgetting the service he had done for her she cried:

'Take away that horrible nutcracker! Take him away!'

The grand marshal of the palace accordingly took poor Nathaniel by the shoulders and pushed him down the stairs. The king, who was very angry at the idea of a nutcracker being offered to him as his son-in-law, raged at the astrologer and Drosselmeyer. Instead of the income of ten thousand thalers a year and the telescope of honour which he had promised the former, instead, also, of the sword set with diamonds, the Order of the Golden Spider, and the new yellow frock-coat which he

should have given to the latter, they were both banished from his kingdom and ordered to be across the frontier within twenty-four hours.

Obedience was essential. Drosselmeyer, the astrologer, and the young Drosselmeyer (now a nutcracker in reality) left the capital and quitted the country. But when night came the two learned men consulted the stars again and read in them that, deformed as he might be, Nathaniel would nonetheless become a prince and a king, unless indeed he chose to remain a private individual, and this was left to his own choice. All this was to happen when his deformity should disappear and that would occur when he had commanded an army in battle, when he had killed the king of the mice who was born after Dame Souriçonne's first seven sons had been killed, and, lastly, when a beautiful lady should fall in love with him.

But while awaiting this brilliant destiny, Nathaniel Drosselmeyer, who had left his father's shop as the only son and heir, now returned to it in the form of a nutcracker. It is needless to say that his father did not recognize him, and when Christopher Zachariah asked his brother and the astrologer what had become of his dearly beloved son, those two illustrious persons replied, with all that self-possession of learned men, that the king and the queen would not allow the saviour of the princess to leave them, and that young Nathaniel remained at the court covered with glory and honour.

As for the unfortunate nutcracker, who felt deeply about his situation, he said not a word but resolved to await patiently the change which some day would take place in him. Nevertheless, it must be said that in spite of his natural good nature he was extremely angry with his uncle who had arrived so unexpectedly and lured him away by so many fine promises, and was the cause of his misfortunes.

And that is the story of the Krakatuk nut and Princess Pirlipatine, and it can be well understood why people often say when speaking of something difficult to do: 'That's a hard nut to crack.'

~ *Chapter Eleven* ~

The months, and then the years went by, and during all this time Marie still had her dreams.

She was persuaded that all that her godfather Drosselmeyer had related was not simply a story but the true history of the disagreement between the nutcracker and the late Dame Souriçonne and her son, the reigning king of the mice. She therefore felt in her heart that the nutcracker could be none other than Nathaniel Drosselmeyer of Nuremberg, the amiable but enchanted nephew of her godfather—she had never doubted that from the moment when he introduced his yellow frock-coat into his story. This belief was strengthened when she found him losing first his hair by sunstroke, and then his eye by an arrow, events which had made necessary the invention of the ingenious glass wig and the black patch.

'But why didn't your uncle help you, poor nutcracker?' she said as she stood at the cupboard gazing up at her favourite. For she remembered that on the success of the battle depended the disenchantment of the little man and his elevation to the rank of king of the kingdom of toys.

'And yet,' she went on, 'although you are unable to move and cannot say a single word to me, I am quite sure, my dear Mr. Drosselmeyer, that you understand me perfectly and that you are well aware of my good intentions towards you. Reckon, then, upon my support when you need it, and in the meantime do not vex yourself.'

In spite of the eloquence of this little speech the nutcracker did not move an inch, but it seemed to Marie that a soft sigh came from behind the glass and that a small voice said:

'Dear Marie, you are my guardian angel. I will be yours and you will be mine.'

Twilight had now come, and the judge returned home accompanied by Doctor Drosselmeyer. Soon everyone was gathered around the table, and in a pause in the conversation Marie turned to the doctor and said:

'I know, godfather, that my nutcracker is your nephew Nathaniel. He has become a prince, and you know that he is at war with the king of the mice. Tell me why you did not help him when you were sitting on top of the clock. And why do you now desert him?'

Then, with a strange smile, her godfather replied:

'My dear, you do not know what you are doing in taking up so warmly the cause of your nutcracker. The king of the mice, who knows that he killed his mother, will persecute him in every way he can. But, in any case, remember that it is not I, but you alone, who can save him. Be strong and faithful, and all will go well.'

Neither Marie nor anyone else understood Doctor Drosselmeyer's words, and they seemed so strange to the judge that he took the doctor's wrist, felt his pulse for some moments in silence, and then said:

'My friend, you are very feverish and should go home to bed.'

That night Marie, who now slept in her mother's room, had fallen asleep. The moon was shining in all its splendour, its rays coming through openings in the curtains. Then she started dreaming. She thought that she had heard a noise that seemed to have come from a corner of the room and which was a mingling of scratching, and little sharp squeaks.

'Oh, dear!' she cried, for she remembered to have heard the same noises at the time of the famous battle. 'The mice are coming again!'

But her voice was stifled in her throat; she tried to get up to run out of the room, but despite how much she tried she could not move her legs. At last, looking towards the corner of the room, she was startled to see the king of the mice scratching for himself a way through the wall, and thrusting in first one of his heads, then another, then a third, and so on until the whole seven, each with a crown, appeared. When he was finally in the room he marched several times around it, rather like a victor over the land he had conquered. Then he said:

'Hi! Hi! Hi! Little girl, you must give me all your sugar-plums and marzipan fruits or else I will eat up your nutcracker.'

With that he vanished through the hole he had made.

Marie was frightened, and when she woke up in the morning she saw that she must do as she was ordered. Accordingly, that evening she put the sugar-plums and marzipan fruits on the ledge of the cupboard.

Next morning the judge's wife said:

'I really don't know where all the mice have suddenly come from in this house. They have actually eaten up all of Marie's sugar-plums.'

She was not quite right, for what had happened was that what had been put out was only spoiled; the gluttonous king of the mice had not found the plums and marzipan quite to his taste, but had nibbled them so badly that they had to be thrown away.

The following night Marie was again awakened by the sound of whinings and squeakings close beside her. It was the king of the mice again, and this time he said:

'You must give me your treasures made of sugar, and some biscuits, or else I will eat up your friend the nutcracker.'

And he went skipping away, disappearing through his hole in the wall.

In the morning Marie, very upset, went straight to the cupboard.

'Alas,' she said, as she turned towards the nutcracker, 'what would I not do for you, Mr. Drosselmeyer? But you must admit that you are making things very hard for me.'

At these words the nutcracker put on such a piteous face that Marie, who imagined that she was forever seeing the jaws of the king of the mice open to devour him, determined to make this second sacrifice to save the unfortunate young man. That evening, therefore, she put her sugar shepherds and shepherdesses (but not before kissing them) and the biscuits on the ledge, together with the sugar sheep.

'Now, really this is too much!' her mother exclaimed next morning.

'These frightful mice must have taken up their dwelling in the cupboard, for all of Marie's sugar figures have been eaten up.'

It was then that Fritz remembered that their baker had an excellent grey cat which would soon put a finish to the mice, but his mother would not hear of it. And then a mousetrap was suggested, at which everyone laughed, for the children's godfather had invented them. But no such thing as a mousetrap could be found in the house, so a servant was sent to Doctor Drosselmeyer, who sent one back. This was baited with a piece of bacon and put in the place where the mice had caused such havoc.

Marie went to bed hoping that in the morning she would find the king of the mice a prisoner in the box, to which his gluttony would almost certainly lead him. But at about eleven o'clock she was again awakened.

'I laugh at the trap! I laugh at the trap!' sang the king of the mice. 'I will not go into the little house, for the bacon doesn't tempt me. But you must give me your picture-books and your silk dress. If you don't I will eat up your friend the nutcracker.'

It can be well imagined how very sad Marie was when she woke in the morning. Her mother told her nothing new when she said that the trap was empty. When she was alone Marie went to the cupboard and said:

'My dear good Mr. Drosselmeyer, where will all this end? When I have given my picture-books to the king of the mice to tear up, and my silk dress which was given to me by my guardian angel to be bitten into little pieces, he will not be content. And when I have nothing else left to give him what can I do, dear good Mr. Drosselmeyer?'

While Marie was saying this, and she was weeping a little, she saw that the nutcracker had a tiny fleck of blood on his neck. From the day that she had discovered that her favourite was the son of a toy-merchant and the nephew of the doctor she had left off carrying him in her arms, and had neither kissed nor cuddled him. Indeed, so great was her shyness, that she had not even dared to touch him with the tip of her finger. But at this moment, thinking that he had been hurt and fearful lest the wound might be dangerous, she lifted him gently out of the cupboard and began to wipe away with her handkerchief this fleck of blood.

But imagine her astonishment when she suddenly felt the nutcracker move about in her hands. She quickly put him back on the shelf. His lips quivered from ear to ear, and this made his mouth seem larger still. He tried hard to speak and after much effort uttered the following words:

'Ah, very dear Miss Silberhaus—excellent friend to me—what do I not owe you—and how grateful I am to you—do not sacrifice for me your picture-books and silk dress—but get me a sword—a good sword—and I will take care of the rest.'

The nutcracker would have said more, but his words became unintelligible and his voice faded away. His eyes, for a moment animated by the greatest sadness, became motionless and vacant.

Marie was not alarmed. On the contrary, she jumped for joy, for she was very happy at the idea of being able to save the nutcracker without having to give up her books and her dress. Only one thing worried her, and that was where she could find the good sword that the little man needed. She decided to explain her difficulty to Fritz.

She took him close to the cupboard and told him all that happened between the nutcracker and the king of the mice. He believed her and said:

'This nutcracker seems to be a brave fellow and I think that I can help him. I have just put a veteran major of the cuirassiers on half-pay for he has finished his time in the service, and I don't think he needs his sword any longer. And it is an excellent sword, too.'

It now only remained to find the major. He was found living on his half-pay in a little tavern which stood in a dark corner on the third shelf of the cupboard. He offered no objection to giving up his sword, and it was immediately hung about the nutcracker's neck.

That night Marie could not go to sleep, and she was very wide awake when she heard the clock strike twelve in the room where the cupboard was. Scarcely had the last stroke sounded when the strange noises came from the direction of the cupboard. Then there was a great clashing of swords as if two enemies were fighting in mortal combat. Suddenly, one of the duellists gave a squeak.

'The king of the mice!' cried Marie, full of joy and terror at the same time.

Then there was dead silence. But presently someone knocked gently, very gently, at her door and a soft, piping voice said:

'Dearest Miss Silberhaus, I have wonderful news for you. Open the door, I entreat you.'

Marie recognized young Mr. Drosselmeyer's voice. She quickly put on a dressing-gown and opened the door. The nutcracker was there holding the blood-stained sword in his right hand and a candle in the other. The moment he saw Marie he knelt on one knee and said:

'It is you alone, my dear young lady, who has given me the courage and the strength to fight that insolent wretch who dared to threaten you. The vile king of the mice is dead. Will you accept these trophies of victory, trophies that are offered by the hand of a knight who is devoted to you until death?'

And with these words the nutcracker drew from his left arm the seven golden crowns of the king of the mice which he had placed there as if they were bracelets and which he now offered to Marie, who accepted them joyfully. The nutcracker, encouraged by her friendliness, then stood up and spoke as follows:

'Dear Miss Silberhaus, now that I have conquered my enemy, what beautiful things I can show you if you will agree to follow me a little way. Don't refuse me, I implore you.'

Marie didn't hesitate for a moment.

'I will follow you, Mr. Drosselmeyer,' she said, 'but you mustn't take me very far, nor keep me long away, for I haven't slept a wink.'

'I shall choose the shortest, although it may be the more difficult, path,' he answered.

And saying this he walked away with Marie following him.

~ *Chapter Twelve* ~

They both soon arrived at a large old cupboard which stood in a passage near the door, and which was used for hanging clothes. There the nut-cracker stopped and Marie saw, to her great astonishment, that the doors of the cupboard which were nearly always kept shut were now open, so that she could see clearly her father's travelling-cloak which was lined with fox-skin and which was spread over the other clothes.

Very skilfully the nutcracker climbed up the cloak by clinging to the braiding and reached the big cape which, held by a loop, fell over the back of the cloak. From under the cape he pulled out a folding ladder made of cedar, which he manoeuvred in such a way that the foot touched the bottom of the cupboard, the top being lost in the sleeve of the cloak.

'And now, my dear,' the nutcracker said, 'be good enough to take my hand so that I can help you to climb up.'

Marie obeyed, and scarcely had she started climbing the ladder than there was a brilliant light and she suddenly found herself transported into the midst of a fragrant meadow which glittered as if it were strewn with precious stones.

'Oh, how beautiful!' Marie cried, dazzled by the sight. 'But where are we?'

'We are in the field of sugar-candy. But unless you want to we'll not stay here . . . You come with me, and we'll go through this gate.'

Then, when Marie raised her eyes she saw a beautiful gate through which they left the field. The gate seemed to be of white, red and blue marble, but when she had come closer she saw that it was actually made of orange peel, raisins and burnt almonds.

The gate opened into a large room, the roof of which was supported by pillars of barley-sugar. In this room there were five monkeys, all dressed in red, and playing music which, if not the most melodious in the world, was at least the most original. Marie was in such a hurry to see more that she did not realize she was walking on pistachio nuts and macaroons which she had, again, mistaken for marble.

After they had passed through the room and had hardly reached the open air she found herself breathing the most lovely scents which came from a delightful little forest that appeared in front of her. This forest was lit up so brilliantly by lanterns that it was easy to see the golden and silver fruit hanging from the branches on ribbons.

'Oh, my dear Mr. Drosselmeyer,' Marie exclaimed, 'what is the name of this charming place?'

'We are now in the forest of Christmas,' was the reply, 'and it is to here that people come to get the trees on which the presents sent by guardian angels are hung.'

'Can't I stay here for a while, for everything is so lovely?'

At that the nutcracker clapped his hands and a number of shepherds and shepherdesses, hunters and huntresses, came out of the forest, all so delicate and white that they seemed to be made of castor sugar. They were carrying an armchair made of chocolate encrusted with angelica, upon which they put a cushion, and politely invited Marie to sit down. She had just done so when, as in ballets, the shepherds and shepherdesses, the huntresses and some of the hunters, took up their places and began to dance to the accompaniment of horns which the rest of the hunters blew with such fervour that their faces became flushed. Then, the dance being finished, the whole troupe disappeared behind a grove of trees.

'You must forgive me, dear Miss Silberhaus,' said the nutcracker, holding out his hand to Marie, 'for having shown you such poor ballet-dancers, but these simpletons can do nothing better than repeat over and over again the same steps. As for the hunters, they blew their horns as if they were afraid of them. I shall be having words with them all.'

'I found everything very delightful,' Marie replied, 'and I hope that

64

you will not be too severe with them.'

The nutcracker made a face as if to say, 'We shall see.'

They then continued their journey and reached a river which seemed to give forth the sweetest of scents.

'This,' said the nutcracker without even waiting to be questioned by Marie, 'is the river of orange juice. It is one of the smallest in the kingdom and, in so far as its scent goes, it cannot compare with the river of lemonade which flows into the southern sea or, as it is sometimes called, the sea of punch. The lake of syrup is also finer and from it run streams into the northern sea, also called the sea of milk of almonds.'

Not far away was a small village in which the houses, the church and the vicarage were all brown. The roofs, however, were gilt, and the walls were resplendent with inlays of red, blue and white sugar-plums.

'This is the village of marzipan,' said the nutcracker. 'As you can see, it is a pretty little place and through it runs the little stream of honey. The people who live here are handsome, but they are always short-tempered because they suffer from toothache a great deal. But, my dear Miss Silberhaus, don't let us stop at all the villages and small towns of the kingdom, let's hurry on to the capital.'

Still holding Marie's hand the nutcracker walked on more briskly. She, full of curiosity and light as a bird, kept up with him. In a few minutes the scent of roses filled the air, and everything about them seemed rose-tinted. Marie noticed that this was the perfume and re-flection from the river of essence of roses which rippled melodiously along. On its waters silver swans with golden collars floated gently about, and diamond fish leapt from the water about them.

The nutcracker clapped his hands again and at once the river of essence of roses began to rise before their eyes, and from its swelling waters there came forth a gondola made of shells and studded with precious stones that glittered in the sun. It was pulled by golden dolphins, and a dozen charming little Moors, wearing caps made from the scales of goldfish and clothes of humming-birds' feathers, jumped on to the bank. They first gently carried Marie and then the nutcracker on to the gondola, which at once started sailing across the river.

It was a ravishing spectacle and one which might be compared to the voyage of Cleopatra—the golden dolphins tossed their heads and threw into the air the glistening drops of water which fell in showers of all the colours of the rainbow. Then soft music began to echo around and silvery voices were heard singing:

'Who are you, thus floating where essence of rose
In a stream of perfume deliciously flows?
Are you the fairies' queen?
Speak, little fishes that gleam in the tide,
Or speak, you cygnets that gracefully glide
Upon the flood serene.'

And all the time the little Moors, who stood behind the seat on the gondola of shells, shook their parasols hung with bells so that their ringing formed an accompaniment to the song. Marie leant over the water, each ripple as it passed reflecting her happy smile.

Thus they crossed the river of essence of roses and reached the bank on the other side. When they were within a short distance from the shore the little Moors jumped, some into the water, others on to the bank, to form a chain to carry Marie and the nutcracker ashore.

The nutcracker now led Marie through a grove, which was perhaps even lovelier than the forest of Christmas so brilliantly did each tree shine and so sweetly did they all smell, each with its own different scent. But what was most remarkable was the quantity of fruit hanging on the branches, some yellow as topaz, others red like the ruby, but all of a wondrous perfume.

'We are now in the wood of preserved fruits,' the nutcracker said, 'and beyond it is the capital.'

When Marie pushed aside the last branches she was stupefied at the magnificence, the size, and the novel appearance of the city which rose before her on a flower-covered plain. The walls and steeples glittered with the most splendid colours, the ramparts and the gates were built of candied fruits which shone in the sun, all rendered more brilliant still by the crystallized sugar that covered them. At the main gate, which was the one by which they entered, silver soldiers presented arms to them, and a little man in a dressing-gown of gold brocade threw himself into the nutcracker's arms, saying:

'Oh, dear prince, have you come at last? Welcome, welcome, to Confituremberg!'

Marie was rather astonished at the grand title given to the nutcracker, but she was soon distracted by the noise of voices chattering around her. So she asked the nutcracker if there was some disturbance or festival in the capital of the kingdom of toys.

'Dear Miss Silberhaus, there is nothing unusual going on. The capital is a happy place and its people are so full of joy that they are always talking and laughing. But do let us keep walking, I implore you.'

Marie, urged by her own curiosity and by the nutcracker's polite invitation, quickened her steps and soon found herself in a large market-place. All the houses surrounding it were made of sugar with fretwork balconies, and in the middle was an enormous sponge-cake from the inside of which played four fountains, of lemonade, orangeade, syrup, and blackcurrant juice. The basin was filled with whipped cream, so delicious looking that a number of well-dressed people were eating from it with spoons. But the most agreeable and amusing part of the whole scene was the crowd of little folk who walked about arm in arm in their thousands, laughing, singing and chattering at the tops of their voices. Marie could now account for all the noise she had heard. Besides those who lived in the capital there were visitors—Armenians, Jews, Greeks, Tyrolese, officers, soldiers, clergymen, monks, shepherds, Punches, jugglers and jumping-jacks.

Soon the noise redoubled at the entrance of a street into the market-place, and the people stood aside to allow a cavalcade to pass. It was the Great Mogul who was being borne on a palanquin, attended by ninety-three peers of his kingdom and seven hundred slaves. But at the same time it happened that from the opposite street there appeared the Great Sultan on horseback, followed by three hundred foot-guards. The two sovereigns had always been rivals and, as a consequence, enemies, and this made it impossible for their followers to meet each other without quarrelling.

As may be imagined it was even worse when these two powerful men found themselves face to face. First of all there was considerable confusion from which the ordinary citizens tried to escape, but cries of anger and despair were soon heard, for a gardener in running away had knocked off with the handle of his spade the head of a Brahmin, who was held in great respect. Moreover, the Grand Sultan's horse had trampled on a frightened Punch who had tried to get away from the riot by creeping between the animal's legs. The din was increasing when the gentleman in the gold brocade dressing-gown who had greeted the nutcracker with the title of 'prince' at the city's gate, leapt with a single bound to the top of the sponge-cake, and having rung a silver sweet-toned bell three times, cried out three times:

'Confectioner! Confectioner! Confectioner!'

The tumult at once subsided and the two processions separated. The Grand Sultan was brushed, for he was covered with dust; the Brahmin's head was fixed on again and he was given instructions not to sneeze for three days lest it should fall off once more; and order was restored. Everyone hurried to the fountain to quench their thirsts and to sample the whipped cream.

The nutcracker and Marie continued their walk and eventually reached the front of the palace which shed around a rosy glow and had a hundred elegant towers. The walls were spangled with nosegays of violets, daffodils, tulips and jasmine, which set off strikingly the rose-coloured walls. The great dome in the centre was covered with thousands of gold and silver stars.

'And what do they call this wonderful building?' Marie asked.

'It is the marzipan palace, and is one of the most remarkable buildings in the capital.'

At that moment soft and delightful music could be heard. The gates of the palace opened of their own accord and twelve little pages came out carrying branches of sweet-smelling herbs which were lighted like torches. Their heads were made of pearl, six of them had bodies made of rubies, the six others of emeralds. And they trotted happily along on golden feet.

They were followed by four ladies about the same size as Claire, Marie's new doll. They were all so beautifully dressed that Marie at once recognized them as being princesses of Confituremberg. All four on seeing the nutcracker hurried to embrace him with the greatest tenderness, exclaiming with one voice:

'Oh, prince, dear prince! Dear, dear brother!'

The nutcracker seemed to be much moved. He wiped away a tear or two and, taking Marie by the hand, said tenderly:

'My dear sisters, this is Miss Marie Silberhaus, whom I present to you. She is the daughter of Judge Silberhaus of Nuremberg, a very great gentleman. It is this young lady who saved my life; first at the moment when I had lost the battle, she threw her shoe at the king of the mice—and again, afterwards, she lent me the sword of a major who was on half-pay—if it were not for her I should now be lying in my grave or, worse still, have been eaten by the king of the mice.'

And turning to Marie he said with an enthusiasm he could barely control:

'Ah, my dear Miss Silberhaus, Pirlipatine although the daughter of a king would not be worthy enough to tie up your shoe-laces.'

'No, no, certainly not!' repeated the four princesses in chorus. And throwing their arms around Marie's neck, they cried:

'You have freed our dear and much-loved prince, excellent Miss Silberhaus!'

Then the princesses led the nutcracker and Marie into the palace, made them sit down on beautiful little sofas made of cedar covered with golden flowers, saying at the same time that they were going to prepare a meal. They hurried to fetch vases and bowls made of the most delicate Japanese porcelain, as well as silver knives, forks and spoons. They then brought the finest fruits and most delicious sugar-plums that Marie had ever seen, and began to bustle about with the cooking.

Now, as Marie was quite a good cook herself, she wished she could join in with the preparations, and as if her thoughts had been understood, the most beautiful of the princesses handed her a golden dish and said:

'Do, please, stir this sugar-candy for me.'

Marie did as she was asked, and as she stirred, the nutcracker began to relate all his adventures. But strange to say it seemed to Marie that the words of young Drosselmeyer and the noise of the stirring became more and more indistinct. Soon she seemed to be surrounded by a light vapour, which turned into a silvery mist and which spread ever more densely around her so that it hid the nutcracker and the princesses from sight.

Strange songs that reminded her of those she had heard on the river of essence of roses, mingled with increasing murmur of waters, came to her ears. Then Marie thought that waves flowed beneath her, raising her up with their swell. She felt as if she was rising high up, higher and higher, then higher still, when, suddenly, she fell from a height she could not measure.

70

~ *Chapter Thirteen* ~

One doesn't fall a great many feet without waking, and thus it was that Marie awoke and on waking she found herself in her own bed. It was broad daylight and her mother was standing beside her. Marie told her just what you have read, and when she had finished, her mother said:

'You have had a very long and charming dream, but now that you are awake you must forget it all and come and have your breakfast.'

Marie began to see that she had to give some proof of the truth of the adventures she had related, and so she went and brought a little box in which she had put the bracelets.

'Here, mother are the seven crowns of the king of the mice which the nutcracker gave me last night as proof of his victory.'

The judge's wife, full of surprise, took them. They were made from an unknown but very bright metal and were made with a delicacy of which human hands were incapable. The judge, himself, could not take his eyes off them. At that moment the door opened and Doctor Drosselmeyer made his appearance. When he was told about the bracelets he burst out laughing and said:

'Well, really this is too good! These are the seven crowns which I used to wear on my watch-chain a great many years ago and which I gave to Marie on her second birthday! Don't you remember?'

The judge and his wife could not recollect anything about the present, but they could not do other than believe the doctor. Marie then went to him and said:

'But you know all about it, godfather. Why don't you admit that the nutcracker is your nephew and that it was he who gave me the seven crowns?'

Doctor Drosselmeyer did not seem to like what he had heard, and he became rather gloomy.

Marie dared not speak any more of her adventures. Nevertheless, the memory of the kingdom of toys was always with her, and when she thought of it all she felt as if she were still in the forest of Christmas, or on the river of essence of roses, or in the city of Confituremberg.

One day when the doctor, with his wig on the floor beside him, the tip of his tongue sticking out from the corner of his mouth, and the sleeves of his coat turned up, was mending a clock it happened that Marie, who was sitting by the cupboard looking at the nutcracker and buried in her own thoughts, suddenly said:

'Oh, my dear Mr. Drosselmeyer, if you were not a little man made of wood as my father says you are, and if you really were alive, I would not, as Princess Pirlipatine did, desert you because you had ceased to be a handsome young man, for I love you dearly.'

Scarcely had she said this when there was such a noise in the room that Marie fell off her chair as if she had fainted. A little later she found herself in her mother's arms who said:

'How is it possible that a big girl like you can be so foolish as to fall off a chair, and just at the very moment when young Mr. Drosselmeyer has arrived at Nuremberg. Come, wipe your eyes and be a good girl.'

Indeed, just as soon as Marie had finished wiping her eyes the door opened and her godfather, with his glass wig on his head, his hat under his arm, and wearing his yellow frock-coat, entered the room. He was smiling, and held by the hand a young man who, although quite small, was very handsome. The young fellow was wearing a superb frock-coat of red velvet embroidered with gold, white silk stockings, and shoes most brilliantly polished. He had a buttonhole and his hair, powdered and braided, hung down behind his neck. The sword that he carried at his side was bright with precious stones, and the hat which he carried was of the finest silk.

Scarcely had he entered the room than he placed at Marie's feet a lot of lovely toys, and better still, marzipan and sugar-plums, the finest she had ever tasted except in the kingdom of toys. When the time came to

eat, and dessert was brought to the table, the amiable young man cracked nuts for everyone and even the very toughest held no worry for him. He simply put them in his mouth with his right hand, jerked his hair from behind with his left, and, crack! the shell was broken.

Marie had blushed when she first met this good-looking fellow, and she blushed deeper still when, after dessert, he invited her to go with him to the room where the glass cupboard stood.

'Yes, go, children,' said Doctor Drosselmeyer. 'I don't want that room any more today as all my friend's clocks are now going well.'

Young Mr. Drosselmeyer had been alone with Marie for a very brief time when he knelt on one knee and spoke to her.

'My dear Miss Silberhaus, you see kneeling before you the happy Nathaniel Drosselmeyer whose life you saved on this spot. You said that you would not have rebuffed me, as Princess Pirlipatine did, if in doing you a great service I became ugly. Now, as the spell which Dame Souriçonne cast upon me was destined to lose all its power on the day when, in spite of my ugliness, I should be loved by a young and beautiful girl, I at that moment ceased to be a stupid nutcracker and resumed my proper appearance which, as you may have noticed, is not disagreeable. So, my dear young lady, if you still have the same feelings towards me, will you marry me and share my throne and my crown, and reign with me over the kingdom of toys of which I have now become the sovereign?'

Then Marie gently raised Nathaniel, saying:

'You are a lovable and good king, and as you have, indeed, a delightful kingdom adorned with magnificent palaces and very happy subjects, I accept you as my future husband—always providing that my parents give their consent.'

The door had opened very gently without the two young people hearing, so preoccupied were they, and the judge and his wife, and godfather Drosselmeyer, walked towards them saying, 'Excellent!' with all their might, which made Marie as red as a cherry. But Nathaniel was not one bit disconcerted. He stepped over to Marie's parents, bowed gracefully, paid them his compliments, and asked if he could marry Marie. His request was at once granted.

That same day Marie became engaged to Nathaniel Drosselmeyer on the condition that the marriage should not take place for a year.

So, in a year's time, the bridegroom came to fetch his bride in a little carriage of mother-of-pearl encrusted with gold and silver, and drawn by ponies no larger than sheep, which were of incalculable value because there were none others like them in the whole world. The young king took his bride to the palace of marzipan where they were married by the chaplain. Twenty-two thousand little people, all covered with pearls, diamonds and other precious stones, danced at the wedding reception.

Even now Marie is still queen of that beautiful country where may be seen the forest of Christmas, the rivers of orangeade, syrup, and essence of roses, diaphanous palaces built of sugar whiter than snow and as transparent as ice—in a word, all kinds of miraculous and wonderful things may be seen there by those who have eyes sharp enough to discover them.

74